Note to Readers

While the Fisk and Stevenson families are fictional, many events in this story actually happened. The centennial, or hundredth birthday, of America was a time of struggle. Many battles took place between the cavalry and Native Americans. Treaties were made and broken. Women, children, and the elderly on both sides were killed.

Immigrants from European nations such as Sweden, Germany, and Ireland worked to build new homes for themselves. For several years, grasshoppers wiped out farmers' crops in the rural areas of Minnesota. Governor Pillsbury, whose family founded the Pillsbury Company that still produces flour, cake mixes, and other food, proclaimed a day of prayer and fasting so that people could repent of their sins and ask God to end the grasshopper plague.

The South had not recovered from the War Between the States, and freed slaves struggled to survive in the face of terrible discrimination. With all these difficulties, people like Bishop Whipple and Chief Joseph worked to make the United States a nation of justice and liberty for all.

CENTENNIAL CELEBRATION

JoAnn A. Grote

BARBOUR
PUBLISHING, INC.
Uhrichsville, Ohio

© MCMXCVIII by Barbour Publishing, Inc.

ISBN 1-57748-287-5

Published by Barbour Publishing, Inc.
P.O. Box 719
Uhrichsville, Ohio 44683
http://www.barbourbooks.com

 Member of the
Evangelical Christian
Publishers Association

Printed in the United States of America.

Cover illustration by Peter Pagano.
Inside illustrations by Adam Wallenta.

CHAPTER 1
Custer's Cavalry

MINNEAPOLIS, MINNESOTA
JUNE 1876

Walter Fisk frowned down at the bolts of material piled high on the square wooden table in the middle of Johnson's Mercantile. His aunt Tina rolled out a bolt of bright blue cloth and held it up to catch the rays of sunlight streaming through the large store windows.

"What do you think of this for your centennial parade blouse, Polly?" she asked.

His cousin Polly's green eyes sparkled and her brown curls bounced as she nodded her head in excitement. "That's perfect!" She grabbed the material and held it up against her dress. "Don't you think so, Walter?"

"Wonderful." She's only going to be part of a flag, he thought. No one will even notice her with the thirty-seven other girls and boys making up the stars in the country's flag. He didn't say so, though. Polly might be only nine and a girl besides, but she'd been pretty nice to him since he and his family had moved to Minneapolis from Cincinnati two weeks earlier.

"Can I have a blouse, too, Aunt Tina?" Seven-year-old Judith tugged at the end of her reddish-brown braid. Her green eyes, so like Polly's, were large and pleading.

"Certainly, and Abe, too. After all, you're both going to be stars in the parade."

Judith and Abe grinned at each other.

"Can I look around the store, Aunt Tina?" Walter asked.

He barely waited for her to say yes before hurrying toward the toy department.

He groaned when Abe and Judith tore around him, almost tripping him. "We're coming with you," his little sister announced.

He got tired of the twins hanging around him all the time. "There's lots of toys to look at." He pointed to a wall of shelves filled with dolls. "Look at those, Judith."

Judith stopped in her tracks. "Ooooh!" A moment later she was darting through the aisles toward the shelves.

"Dolls!" Abe rolled his eyes, but took off after Judith.

Walter grinned. The Terrible Twins weren't really twins. They weren't even brother and sister. They were cousins. Judith was his little sister, and Abe was Polly's little brother. Everyone called them twins because they'd been born on the same day—Judith in Cincinnati and Abe in Minneapolis.

6

They didn't look alike, either. Instead of reddish-brown hair and green eyes like Judith, Abe had curly brown hair like his father's and brown eyes like Walter's.

They weren't even terrible, Walter admitted to himself, just pesty and noisy.

The first thing in the toy department to catch Walter's eye was a shiny black tin train engine. Now here was something for a ten-year-old boy to get excited about!

He picked up the engine and looked it over carefully, noticing all the details. The round smokestack rose from the top. A large piece of glass protected the huge kerosene lantern that hung in the front above the windows so that the engineers could see what was ahead of them on the track and so people could see the train coming. There was even a string attached to the black iron bell on top of the train. The sound of the bell also let people know the train was coming.

In tiny letters on the side, the word "Hiawatha" was painted. Walter remembered that train engines weren't being named anymore. Instead they were being given numbers. He thought he liked the names better.

"Is that like the engine your father drives?" Polly asked.

Walter almost jumped at the sound of her voice. He looked down at her. He was tall and skinny, and she looked very short and plump beside him.

"It's not *just* like Father's engine," he said. "No two engines are exactly the same, but this is a lot like the one Father drives. It's like the one we rode on from Cincinnati."

Polly sighed and picked up a tin passenger car. "It would be fun to ride on a train and see the country and towns pass by your windows. You must have seen so much on your trip!"

"It was fun," Walter admitted, feeling a bit proud. After

all, not every ten-year-old boy had ridden that far on a train and seen so much of the United States of America.

"Your father has the best job in the world," Polly said. "Just think of seeing new places and different people every day."

"Sometimes he takes me along, when I'm not in school."

Polly's eyes grew huge. "Do you think he'd take me along, too?"

"Maybe. I can ask him." No wonder Polly thought it sounded like so much fun. Her father, Walter's uncle Enoch, was a banker in one of Minneapolis's tall new brick buildings. He went to work in the same building every day. The bank was on the first floor, which was a good thing for Uncle Enoch. He'd lost a leg in the War Between the States, and it was hard for him to climb stairs.

Polly's mother stopped behind them. "Would you two round up the Terrible Twins and meet me at the counter?"

A short round man with gray-blond hair and pale blue eyes stood behind the counter when the children reached the front of the store. "Can I get anything else for you today, Mrs. Stevenson?"

"No, Mr. Johnson."

Mr. Johnson measured the amount of material Aunt Tina needed and cut it. While he folded it and wrapped it in brown paper, Aunt Tina asked about his family.

"Well, you know, Mrs. Stevenson, my son is with the cavalry. He's with General Custer's regiment." The man shook his head. Walter could tell he wasn't happy about his son being in the cavalry. He'd heard a lot of the cavalry's men were people who had come to America from other countries and couldn't find work. He wondered if the clerk's son was one of them.

Aunt Tina shook her head and clucked her tongue. "I hope the rumors of the Indians planning a war this summer aren't true."

Mr. Johnson heaved a sigh that lifted the gold watch chained across the front of his vest. "Yah, but I'm sure there will be trouble on the frontier. People will look for gold in the Black Hills and cross the Indians' lands, no matter what the government says."

Walter had to listen hard to understand him. There were many Scandinavian immigrants living in the area, and most of them talked in that same sing-song tone and pronounced words funny. They usually said "w" and "wh" sounds with a "v" sound, he'd learned, and said "yah" instead of yes. He wondered why they had trouble pronouncing words right!

A large woman standing beside Aunt Tina plunked down a new kerosene lamp on the counter. "Humph! I don't know why the Indians should mind the miners and settlers. There's so much land in the Dakotas and farther west that there's room for everyone and land to spare for hundreds of years."

Mr. Johnson looked at her over the top of his spectacles. "Yah, but the Indians don't think so."

The woman stuck her chin in the air. "If the Indian wars do come, those savages deserve whatever happens to them. Our cavalry will show them how to behave toward white people."

Walter shifted his feet and scowled at the lady. Why should a woman in Minneapolis hate the Indians so? He didn't think there were any Indians left in this area. Even if there were, why shouldn't she respect them, like she would anyone else?

He glanced at Aunt Tina and Mr. Johnson, expecting one

of them to tell the woman that Indians weren't savages. Instead Mr. Johnson looked more worried than ever and nodded. "Yah. I hope my son doesn't have to fight them in battle."

Walter was glad when Mr. Johnson had tied Aunt Tina's package with twine, it was paid for, and they could leave. He didn't want to hear any more mean talk about the Indians, but children weren't supposed to tell adults when they thought they were wrong.

"May I show Walter around town a bit before going home, Mother?" Polly asked.

Aunt Tina tilted her head and scrunched her eyebrows together. "What part of town are you planning to show him?"

"Just some of the places nearby."

"All right, as long as you stay away from the riverside."

"We will, Mother."

"See you get home soon and do your chores. I expect Walter has chores to do this afternoon, too."

Walter and Polly nodded. There were always chores to do!

"Can we go, too?" Abe asked.

"Yes, can we?" Judith chimed in.

Aunt Tina hesitated, then gave Polly and Walter a smile. "Not this time. You can walk home with me."

Walter was glad Polly had asked to show him about town. He'd had to spend most of his time the last couple weeks helping his mother clean the house they'd moved into and unpack all the things they'd brought from Cincinnati.

The wind whipped at Walter's straight brown hair and Polly's curls as they walked down Nicollet Avenue with its business buildings on each side of the street. It was one of the busiest streets in the young town, but it seemed like a country street to Walter.

They crossed the street to get to a candy store, weaving in and out between horse-drawn carriages and carts. Walter's shoes scrunched in the mud. When they reached the other side, he scraped the soles of his shoes against the worn wooden sidewalk.

"Why are the streets in Minneapolis all dirt and mud?" he asked. "The streets were paved in Cincinnati."

Polly just laughed. "Cincinnati is much older than Minneapolis. Father says Minneapolis is almost on the edge of the frontier. But at least it wasn't called 'Pig's Eye,' like St. Paul was first called." St. Paul was the city across the river.

Walter burst out laughing. "If St. Paul's streets are as muddy as these, it should still be called Pig's Eye."

Walter had thought moving to a new city would be exciting, but he hadn't realized how much he'd have to learn. Even though the city wasn't as big as Cincinnati, Walter couldn't remember where everything was built. He'd had to learn where the mercantile was, and the grocery store, and the church, and the school.

Polly had been a lot of help to him, showing him places. She showed him the shortcuts, too, that their parents wouldn't take: worn paths through empty lots, broken boards in neighborhood fences, and the yards they could cut through without the owner yelling at them.

"Oh, look, Walter!" Polly grabbed his arm. "There's a streetcar! Aren't they exciting?"

Mud splattered from beneath the huge hooves of the horses pulling the wooden streetcar along wooden rails laid in the street. The car was painted bright colors and had a driver sitting outside in front of it, but otherwise it looked like a passenger car on a train.

"Haven't you ever ridden on a streetcar?"

"No." Polly shook her head, her long red curls shining in the summer sunlight. "We didn't have streetcars until last year. Now we have sixteen."

Walter could hear the pride in her voice and couldn't help trying to top her. "Cincinnati has lots of streetcars and has had them for many years."

Polly opened her mouth, then shut it tight. She started walking quickly. Walter caught up to her easily with his longer legs.

"What's the matter?"

"Why do you always have to find a reason to make Cincinnati sound better than Minneapolis? You aren't going to make any friends if you keep saying how bad it is here."

Walter shrugged. "Cincinnati is one of the biggest cities in the country. Of course it's better."

"There you go again!" Polly kept her gaze straight in front of her.

They walked out of the business section of town and into an area where mostly houses were built. The majority of the houses were white, two stories high, and built of wood. Children played in some of the yards, but they were much younger than Polly and Walter.

Boys' voices raised in play caught Walter's attention. It sounded like a lot of boys, and they were calling and yelling. As Walter and Polly walked, the voices grew louder and Walter's curiosity grew, too.

When they passed the last house on the block, they reached a large empty lot filled with nothing but mud puddles, ankle-high weeds, and boys. Lots of boys! Some of them had sticks they were pretending were swords or pistols or rifles. Others had weapons carved out of wood. Still others were pretending to shoot bows and arrows. It only took Walter a minute to figure out they were playing cavalry and Indians.

Walter thought most of the boys were about his age, though some were younger and some older. His chest ached at the thought of his friends in Cincinnati. If he were back there, he'd be playing baseball with his friends now. He hadn't any new friends in Minneapolis yet.

"Why don't you ask if you can play with them?" Polly asked.

Walter shook his head. "No. I don't know any of them. Do you know them?"

"No, but you can get to know them if you play with them."

Walter stuffed his hands in his pockets and tried to look like he didn't care whether he made new friends. "It's no fun to play with children you don't know."

"How are you going to get to know them if you don't play with them?"

Walter rolled his eyes. "You grew up with your friends or met them at school. What do you know about it?"

"A lot of my friends moved to Minneapolis like you did."

Walter ignored her and watched the boys playing.

Polly yanked on his sleeve and pointed across the lot. "There's Grant. I'm going to go say hello to him."

Polly hurried away. Walter followed her slowly across the edge of the lot, where they wouldn't be in the way of the boys who were playing. A boy about his own age was leaning against a tree at the edge of the lot, watching the boys play, too. He was almost the same height as Walter. His hair was straight and so dark it was almost black.

13

Polly introduced them, and the boys nodded at each other and said hello. When Polly told Grant that Walter was from Cincinnati, Grant's eyes lit up with interest. He asked Walter lots of questions about what life was like there.

"What's your favorite thing to do?" Grant asked finally.

"Play baseball."

"Me, too."

They grinned at each other.

"Grant, will you help us with our parade project?" Polly asked.

"What parade project?"

"For the centennial parade. Absolutely everyone is doing something for the parade except the children, so we decided to do a project."

Grant raised black eyebrows. "If everyone is going to be in the parade, who is going to watch?"

Walter chuckled.

Polly perched fists behind her back. "You know what I meant, Grant La Pierre." As was normal for Polly, she didn't stay upset. "Some of us children are going to make a human flag for the parade. Thirty-eight children with white paper stars on their heads and wearing blue blouses will be stars— one for every state in the country. We have big strips of red and white bunting for the flag's stripes. We need a couple more boys to help carry the stripes. Will you help?"

Grant hesitated.

"She talked me into it already," Walter said.

"All right. I'll do it."

"Thanks!" Polly smiled. "We're practicing at the school grounds tomorrow at 6:30 in the evening."

"I'll be there."

Polly pointed to the children playing cavalry and Indian.

"Do you know these boys, Grant?"

"Some of them."

"They'd probably let you and Walter play with them."

Grant pushed away from the tree and scowled at her. His black eyebrows met above his dark brown eyes. "I don't play cavalry and Indians," he said fiercely.

Without even a good-bye, he turned and stalked down the street.

Walter watched him go with a sinking feeling in his stomach. Grant was the first boy his age he'd met that he liked in Minneapolis. "What upset him so?"

Polly shook her head. "He's like that. He'll be nice and friendly, and all of a sudden he gets moody and leaves. Sometimes I think he has a secret."

What foolishness! Walter thought. What kind of secret could Grant have that would make him act that way? "Let's go home," he said, starting to walk away. Polly followed.

Walter looked back over his shoulder at the boys still playing in the empty lot. Their pretend battle shouts followed Walter down the wooden sidewalk. He wished he'd had the courage to ask to play with them the way Polly had suggested.

He watched Grant hurrying down the sidewalk almost a block in front of them. He hoped he and Grant could be friends someday. Did the other boy really have a secret?

CHAPTER 2
Attacked!

"Pick flowers and make a rope out of them?" Walter snorted in disgust at Brita Swenson's invitation. "Polly can go with you if she wants, but I'll stay home."

Polly frowned at him over Brita's blond head. "You'll only be bored spending the afternoon here. Why don't you come with us?"

"Yes," Brita urged. "All the Swedish people will be there. Maybe you'll meet some boys you know. My brother Per is fourteen. He and his friends love the Midsummer Festival."

Polly grinned. "Besides, the festival lasts until after midnight."

Walter's ears pricked up at that. Then he kicked at the

kitchen rug. "Aw, our parents would never let us stay up that late." He glanced at Brita. "Do your parents let you and Per stay up for the whole celebration?"

Brita's blond braids bounced as she nodded. "Oh, yes! After we set up the *majstang*—I mean, the Maypole—there's dancing and singing." She laughed. "And lots of food."

"If our parents say we may go, will you come?" Polly asked.

Walter nodded slowly. If Per and his friends were going, maybe it would be all right.

Later Walter was quite surprised when both his parents and Polly's gave permission for them to go. They said it was all right because it had been Brita's parents' idea and Mr. and Mrs. Swenson would be watching out for the children.

"At my house are some Swedish outfits you can wear," Brita said, leading the way out the back door.

Half an hour later, Walter frowned down at his colorful vest and the yellow trousers that tied just below his knees over high white socks. Mrs. Swenson had said he was "lucky" that Per had outgrown these clothes!

"I feel like a parrot at a circus," Walter muttered. Then he shrugged. "Oh, well. If Per isn't embarrassed wearing one of these costumes, I guess I can do it."

When Walter entered the parlor, the smell of roses filled the air. The small wild flowers filled vases all around the room. He remembered leafy twigs had been tied about the front door. The rooms didn't have much furniture, but the flowers and greenery made the rooms cheerful.

Almost like Christmas in June, he thought.

Polly and Brita were waiting for him in the parlor. Both were dressed in white blouses, red vests, and an apron striped red, yellow, and green. Brita wore a small, tight-fitting white cap above her blond braids.

"I haven't another cap," she was telling Polly, "but we can make you a crown of roses for your hair when we reach the park."

Polly spotted Walter and twirled around. Her full skirt swirled in the breeze she created. Her eyes sparkled. "Isn't this fun, Walter?"

Walter glanced down at his costume again. His cheeks grew hot, and he knew he was blushing. "It's a silly custom, if you ask me, dressing up in funny old clothes."

The smile left Brita's face and eyes. "I'll see if I can help *Mor* with the food." She started past Walter, but she didn't look at him. She was looking at the floor.

Guilt swept through him. He hadn't meant to hurt her feelings. He'd only been embarrassed to be seen in these clothes. "I'm sorry, Brita," he said as she reached the door.

Brita nodded and kept walking toward the kitchen.

"How could you say something so mean?" Polly hissed angrily. Her hands were balled into fists at her sides.

"I guess I wasn't thinking."

"She's only trying to be nice and share a fun day with us. You're never going to make new friends if you make fun of other people's customs and habits."

Walter knew his cousin was right, but he didn't like having a girl who was a year younger than him tell him the truth. Angry, he hurried outside to wait for the family.

Every member of Brita's family, and Walter and Polly, too, had their arms full of food or flowers when they arrived at the park. Mr. Swenson had a strangely shaped, long leather box under one arm.

Walter soon lost his embarrassment over his clothes. The closer the family came to the park, the more people they saw wearing bright costumes like their own. The park was filled with the bright greens, reds, and yellows.

And the wooden tables were filled with food. "You can't see the table for all the dishes," Polly said.

Walter grinned. He could see plump Polly was eyeing the dessert tables. He had to admit the tarts and cookies looked good. The wonderful smells made his stomach growl.

"Let's go help make flower ropes for the Maypole," Brita said eagerly.

She and Polly ran off toward a group of people working around a large pile of flowers. Walter trudged behind. *This sure isn't my idea of a fun day!* he thought.

He stood behind the girls as they worked wild roses into a long rope. "Is Midsummer Festival a holiday to celebrate flowers?"

Brita and the girls around her laughed. "No, silly."

Walter wanted to sink into the ground. It had been bad enough wearing this stupid outfit. Now a bunch of *girls* were laughing at him because he didn't know what the festival celebrated.

"In northern Sweden in the middle of summer, daylight lasts all night long. That's what the Midsummer Festival celebrates," Brita explained. "That's why we stay up all night, dancing and singing."

"Oh." Walter couldn't imagine the sun staying out all night long. He wondered whether it stayed out all night and set in the morning, or if it stayed out all night and all day both. He didn't ask. He didn't want the girls to laugh at him again.

Instead he said with a grin, "The sun doesn't stay up all night here."

"Wouldn't it be fun if it did?" Brita asked. She sighed, and her flower-filled hands dropped to her aproned lap. "I was born in America, so I've never seen the sun stay up all night. *Mor* has told me about it, though, how wonderful it was and what fun the midsummer celebration was in her town in Sweden. She grew up near the coast, and people danced all night on the harbor docks."

"Hey, Walt." Someone shook his shoulder lightly. He turned to see Per beside him. "You don't want to help the girls with the flowers, do you? You can help us men put the Maypole up after the girls are done decorating it. That's work that takes muscles." He flexed an arm and winked. "Come with me, and I'll show you around."

Per didn't have to ask twice. Walter would much rather spend time with an older boy than with the girls!

Later on, just as Per had promised, he and Walter helped set up the Maypole. Walter thought the decorated pole a rather silly thing, but he'd learned his lesson and didn't say so.

After the pole was up, the music started. Walter and Polly were surprised to see Mr. Swenson open his long leather box and take out a fiddle. Sticking it under his bearded chin, he turned the screws to tune the strings. Then he waxed the hair on his bow. It was only minutes before he and the other men were ready, and cheerful music filled the park.

Walter felt a poke in his arm. He turned to see Polly beside him. "What's that?" she asked, pointing at a nearby tree.

From the tree's low, thick branches hung what looked like large leather bags. Women in costume were hanging more of the bags by their wide leather straps.

Curious, Walter and Polly walked closer.

Polly gasped. "Why, there are babies in the bags!"

Walter rolled his eyes. "Don't be silly."

But as they drew closer, he saw she was right. "They *are* babies!"

20

Behind them, Brita giggled. "Haven't you ever seen a Swedish cradle?"

"Cradle?" Polly stared at her with large eyes.

"Cradles in America are wooden and rock on the floor," Walter said. *Swedes have such strange customs,* he thought.

"Swedes have those kinds of cradles, too," Brita said with a smile.

Walter frowned. "Aren't the mothers afraid the cradles will fall and the babies will get hurt?"

"Mothers often hang the babies in the trees in Sweden, at festivals like this and when they go to church in the summer," Brita explained. "The mothers are careful to hang them on strong branches."

Polly laughed. "Maybe that's where the song 'Rock-a-bye Baby' started." She started singing, and Brita joined in:

"Rock-a-bye, baby,
   in the tree top,
when the wind blows,
   the cradle will rock,
when the bough breaks,
   the cradle will fall,
and down will come baby,
   cradle and all."

Walter rolled his eyes again in disgust as the girls giggled together.

"Oh, it's time for the dancing!" Brita grabbed Polly's hand. "Come on!"

Walter followed the girls. Brita's blond braids bounced against her back as she and Polly dashed for the Maypole.

People, young and old, surrounded the Maypole and

began dancing. They formed two circles. One danced in one direction, and the other circle danced in the opposite direction. Per and his mother joined one of the circles, but Brita stayed to the side with Walter and Polly. The people watching clapped and sang.

It seemed to Walter and Polly that they were the only people in the park that didn't know the words to the songs. At first that made Walter feel uncomfortable, as if everyone was watching him.

Then he thought, *I'm going to have fun, anyway.* He began clapping with everyone else and stamping his feet in time with the music.

Polly and Walter's parents didn't approve of dancing, but the cousins could enjoy listening to the music, anyway.

After the ring dancing was over, the music continued while people ate and talked. Per was busy with his friends and he didn't ask Walter to join them, so Walter stayed with the girls and wished he were with Per instead.

Later Per came over for something to eat. Hoping to keep his attention, Walter said, "Brita told us she was born in America. Were you born here, too?"

Per shook his head. "No, I was born on the ship when my parents made the trip from Sweden to America. That was in 1862."

Mrs. Swenson nodded, her face unusually serious. "The Lord, He was watching over us. There were many storms, but the ship did not sink. Then our first summer, we survived something even more frightening than a storm at sea."

Walter sat up straighter. "What could be scarier than a storm on the ocean?"

Mrs. Swenson's round face grew pale and her eyes large. *"Indians!"*

CHAPTER 3

The Swensons' Tragedy

"Indians!" Mrs. Swenson's hoarse whisper sent a shiver down Walter's spine. He frowned. Why did everyone in Minnesota think Indians were terrible people?

Mrs. Swenson sat on the bench beside the table. Her hands were clenched so tightly in her lap that the knuckles were white. "We moved to land west of Minneapolis along the Minnesota River near New Ulm to farm. My husband and his bachelor brother worked hard to make the land ready to plow and planted a little land. They built a tiny one-room log cabin for us to live in."

Walter saw lines deepen in Mrs. Swenson's wide face. Her eyes stared off into space over his head. He could tell she wasn't hearing the cheerful crowd of Swedish friends

23

who filled the park with their laughter and chatter. She was reliving another time.

Mrs. Swenson went on in a trembling voice. "The men were working in the field. My husband came to the house for a drink of water. We heard his brother scream. Through the window, we saw an Indian kill him."

The hair on Walter's head felt like it stood straight up.

Polly gasped. "How terrible!"

He glanced at Polly. Her eyes were wide, staring at Mrs. Swenson.

"There were other Indians, running through the field toward the house," Mrs. Swenson continued.

"What did you do?" Walter asked, his heart racing.

"We knew there wasn't time to run away and hide. There was a trap door in the cabin leading to a root cellar where we stored vegetables. We hurried down there, hoping they wouldn't find us."

"Did they?" Polly asked. "Were you captured?"

Mrs. Swenson shook her head. "No. They must have been in a hurry and not looked for us carefully, or else they thought we'd left for town, or that Olaf's brother was the only one at that farm. We could hear them hurrying about the cabin, opening cupboards and drawers."

"You must have been horribly scared!" Polly sounded breathless.

"Yes. It was terrible. Per was still a baby. I was so afraid he would start crying and the Indians would hear us."

Per grinned. "Guess I was a pretty smart baby. I knew when not to cry."

Walter and Polly gave shaky little laughs.

Mrs. Swenson rested a chubby, work-worn hand on her son's shoulder. "The Lord protected us. If He hadn't, you and I might not be here now, and Brita would never have been born."

Walter couldn't imagine the world without Brita and Per.

"Why did the Indians attack your farm?" he asked. "Was your farm on their land?"

"It was on land that used to belong to the Indians, but the Indians had sold it," Mrs. Swenson explained.

Per perched on the table beside her. "It wasn't only our farm that was attacked," he said. "The attack was part of the Sioux Uprising."

Walter's brows scrunched together. "What was the Sioux Uprising?"

Per turned to him. "It happened in 1862. There weren't many soldiers left in Minnesota, because they were fighting in the War Between the States. The Sioux Indians, who lived along the Minnesota River, decided it would be a good time for them to have a war and try to get back lands they'd sold to the government and settlers."

"The Indians didn't win," Polly said, interrupting.

"No," Per agreed, "but they hurt and killed many people besides my uncle."

"Yah." Mrs. Swenson nodded, her double chin bobbing. She continued the story. "We waited in the dark, cold root cellar a long time after we thought the Indians left. We were afraid they might be hiding outside, waiting for us. We were cramped and cold. Per was hungry. He started fussing."

Per grinned.

Mrs. Swenson didn't notice. "My husband and I prayed together, very quietly. Then he lifted the trap door and slipped up into the house. Waiting in the dark, I didn't know if Per and I would ever see him alive again."

Walter shivered. What would it have been like to sit in the dark and wonder whether his own father would be killed?

He glanced at Polly. He could see by the horror on her round face that she was wondering the same thing.

"You did see him alive again, though." Polly's voice sounded breathless, like she'd been running a long way.

"Yah. When he came back, we took a little food and water and the rifle and ammunition we had taken to the root cellar. I took the cradle for Per and our family Bible. That was all we could carry, and all we dared take time to pack. It was hard to leave our home and not know whether we would ever be back."

She paused again. Walter held his breath, waiting to hear what happened next. He wanted to tell her to hurry, but that wouldn't have been polite.

Finally she spoke again. "We hurried through the tall prairie grass toward New Ulm. It was the worst night of my life. Fires from burning farms lit the night sky with orange and yellow flames. The air was filled with smoke.

"We found other settlers headed for New Ulm. Their faces all looked the same. Their eyes were large with fear. My husband and I must have looked like that, too. We saw the bodies of many dead settlers along the way."

"More than five hundred settlers were killed," Per explained quietly. "About thirty thousand settlers left their homes."

"Were you safe in New Ulm?" Polly asked Mrs. Swenson.

Mrs. Swenson shook her head. "Not safe, but safer. The Indians attacked the town. There was a terrible battle, but only one white person was killed there."

"Did you ever go back to your farm?" Walter asked.

"Yah. The Indians had burned everything. There was

26

nothing left. We moved to Minneapolis, where Mr. Swenson could find safer work."

Suddenly Mr. Swenson was beside them, smiling. He set his violin on the table and grabbed his wife's hand. "Dance with me, wife," he said with a laugh.

A wide smile chased away the lines the story had furrowed in Mrs. Swenson's face. She hurried across the grass with her husband.

Walter stood where he was, staring at the leather cradles swinging in the night breeze. It was hard to believe Mr. and Mrs. Swenson had been a young couple, attacked by Indians, and left with nothing but a Bible, a baby, and a leather cradle.

No wonder people in Minnesota were frightened of Indians and thought the cavalry should kill them.

Still, wouldn't Mr. Swenson and Per fight for their own country? Wouldn't Walter and his father do the same? Could he blame the Indians for trying to keep the lands that had belonged to them for hundreds, maybe thousands of years?

Sometimes right and wrong weren't as simple as he thought they should be. Were the Swensons right to fear and hate the Indians? Or was Uncle Timothy right to think the Indians were fine people who only lived and believed differently from people like Walter and his family?

Who was right?

CHAPTER 4
Centennial Celebration

Walter brushed aside a long, dusty cobweb hanging from the attic's wooden rafters. Beside him, Grant sneezed.

"Papa said it was in a trunk, right?" Walter looked around. It was almost seven o'clock, and there wasn't much sunlight reaching through the small attic window. The attic was filled with lumps and shadows and shapes, but he wasn't sure what they all were.

"That's what he said," Grant agreed. "An *old* trunk."

"It has to be here somewhere." Walter pushed aside a long, old-fashioned dress that hung beside the brick chimney. He took an impatient step. His foot started to sink. "Hey!" He wobbled, trying to regain his balance.

Grant grabbed his arm. "Did you miss the boards?"

"Yes. I was looking for the trunk so hard that I forgot we could go right through the ceiling if we don't walk on the boards."

Grant grinned. "Your mother wouldn't like that."

It took a couple more minutes and breaking through a lot more cobwebs before they found the trunk. It was old, like Mr. Fisk had said. "It's smaller than I thought it would be," Walter said, kneeling in front of it.

"Oof!" He pushed at the round top. It didn't open. "Pretty heavy."

Grant knelt and shoved at it, too. Together they were able to open it. It was filled to the top with a jumble of items.

"I don't see the flag." Walter started digging through the trunk. His father had said he could hang out the flag for the centennial celebration the next day. "Dad said it's not an up-to-date flag. It has only thirty-seven stars. It should have thirty-eight, since Colorado became a state this year."

Grant grunted. "I don't think anyone will take the time to stop and count the stars, anyway."

Walter chuckled and kept digging. A moment later he pulled out an old book. "What's this?"

He studied it in the dim light. The leather cover was worn and stained. The spine was almost torn off. He could tell there had once been gold lettering on the front, but it was mostly gone now.

The dust tickled his nose as he opened the book. Instead of type-printed words, the pages were filled with hand-written words in a fancy writing style. He set it aside and went back to looking for the flag. A minute later, he found it.

"This is it," he said triumphantly. He slammed down the

cover of the trunk. The boys hurried across the boards and down the ladder to the second floor.

A minute later they joined Walter's and Polly's families in the hot kitchen. They'd gotten together for a taffy pull.

From the iron range where she was stirring something in a heavy cast iron kettle, Polly turned. "There you are! Just in time, too. The taffy is almost ready to pull."

"Great!" Grant said, looking eager to try the candy.

From habit, Walter glanced at the wood box and coal bucket beside the stove. Both still had some fuel in them. It was Walter's job to keep them full. Some days it seemed he spent most of his hours chopping wood in the backyard and hauling buckets of coal from the cellar. He almost hated to see anyone cook anymore; cooking just made more work for him.

But he had to admit, the taffy did smell good—that is, what he could smell of it over the odor of the wood and coal.

Papa was pumping a glass of water at the iron sink. The heavy pump handle squeaked in protest. Water flooded his glass, splashing merrily over the edges and into the sink. "I see you found the flag."

"Yes." Walter held out the book. "We found this, too."

"William's journal! I'd forgotten all about that."

"Who is William, Uncle Charles?" Polly asked.

"Who *was* William, you mean. He was one of your ancestors. He lived in Boston and fought in the Revolutionary War. This is the journal he kept during the war."

Walter and Polly exchanged grins. "You mean our family has been in America since the Revolutionary War?"

"Since before that. Your first ancestors in America came over on the *Mayflower* in 1620."

"In school, we studied about the Pilgrims coming on the *Mayflower*," Polly said, "but I didn't know our ancestors were on that ship. That means our ancestors must have been English."

"Yes. Later, the English ancestors married people who came to America from Ireland," Walter's mother explained. "So you have both English and Irish blood. I believe your green eyes come from your English ancestors, Polly."

A grin filled Brita's face. "All my ancestors are from Sweden."

Everyone laughed. Anyone would know Brita's family was from Sweden. She couldn't keep it a secret with her wide Scandinavian face, dancing blue eyes, pale blond hair, and heavy Swedish accent.

Walter turned to Grant. "What country did your ancestors come from?"

Grant hesitated before answering. "France. My father's grandfather came from France. He was a fur trapper. So was my grandfather. My father was a trapper when he was a young man, but now he works in the city so we can be together."

Walter swaggered a bit. "I guess *our* ancestors were the first to come to America." He couldn't help but feel a bit proud of the fact, especially with the centennial celebration the next day.

"The Indian nations were here first." Grant's voice was quiet, but everyone heard him.

"Sure," Walter agreed, "but that was before the people in Europe found out about America and started coming here and made it one country."

Polly's green eyes sparkled. "We have people in this room from four different countries. Isn't that exciting?"

Aunt Tina grabbed the wooden spoon from Polly's hand.

"You're going to have some excitement on the stove in a minute if you don't pay attention to the taffy. If you stop stirring, it will scorch." She peered into the pan. "Bring me a cup of cold water. I'll see if it's ready to pull."

Polly took a cup from the cup hooks on the open cupboard. Her father pumped cold water into it, and Polly carried it to the stove.

Aunt Tina dribbled a bit of the golden candy into the water, then looked at her daughter. "It's forming a hard little ball. The taffy is ready to pull. Are your hands buttered, everyone?"

Walter reached for the plate of butter sitting in the middle of the wooden kitchen table.

"Wash your hands first, boys," his aunt warned just in time.

Soon there were three sets of taffy being pulled by six sets of hands: Polly and Brita pulled one strand, Walter and Grant pulled another, and Uncle Enoch and Aunt Tina pulled the last.

"Ooch!"

"Ow!"

"Yipes!"

Even with butter on their hands to keep the candy from sticking to their skin, everyone could tell that the candy was hot. They had to keep their hands moving constantly to keep from burning themselves and to keep the candy from cooling too quickly.

Uncle Enoch and Aunt Tina were much faster than the others.

"Let's try to go as fast as them." Grant's eyes gleamed with fun.

Try as they would, the boys couldn't keep up with the

32

adults. Neither could the girls. Still, they all had fun trying. Soon everyone was laughing as they yanked and turned the candy.

The ropes of candy grew long, skinny, and hard. Finally it was cool enough to break off into small pieces and place on platters on the table. They covered them with clean linen dishtowels to keep bugs away from the candy.

"Do you think anyone will buy the taffy?" Brita asked, washing the greasy butter from her hands with strong smelling soap.

"Sure they will," Grant encouraged. "There won't be many stores open during the parade where people can buy food if they get hungry."

"People had better buy it." Polly pumped water into the dirty kettle, then placed the kettle on the stove to heat the water. "I have to pay Mother back for the cloth she bought for our parade flag."

Although he didn't tell her so, Walter was impressed that Polly had come up with the flag idea and found enough children to help with it. Even though she was only nine, she had good ideas and wasn't afraid to ask others for help.

"Can we stay up until midnight, Papa?" Walter asked.

"May we," his mother corrected.

"Yes, may we? I heard the butcher at the meat shop today say some of the neighbor men will shoot firecrackers at midnight."

"Why midnight?" Polly asked.

"Because that's when July Fourth begins, the day of our country's centennial," Walter explained.

Papa grinned and winked at his wife. "You wouldn't want to get me into trouble with your mother, would you? You'd better ask her if you can stay up so late."

Mama crossed her arms over her aproned chest and tried to look stern. She walked slowly past each child, putting her face close to theirs and studying them. Polly giggled. Walter bit his lip to keep from smiling. Mama looked across at Aunt Tina and raised her eyebrows. Aunt Tina nodded.

Finally Mama smiled. "All right. Since this celebration only comes along every one hundred years and none of us are likely to be alive in 1976, you may stay up."

"Yes!" The two cousins started jumping and hollering.

Walter could hardly believe they'd been allowed to stay up so late for two nights—first the Midsummer Festival and now the eve of the centennial.

Mama held up an index finger, and the children stopped. "You can stay up only a few minutes past midnight. Remember, you must be at the starting point for the parade at eight in the morning."

"And I have to be at the station at four-thirty," Papa reminded them. "A lot of people from the nearby towns and countryside plan to take the trains in to Minneapolis for the celebration."

"Do you have everything ready for the parade, Polly?" Mama asked her niece.

"Yes, ma'am."

"Let's go outside where it's cooler," Walter suggested. The kitchen was still hot from the stove, even though the windows were open.

The early July day had been hot and hadn't cooled down much, even though the sun was almost set. It was twilight, that pretty time of day when it's not quite dark and the world is growing quiet, except for the hum of evening insects.

"Ouch!" Walter slapped at a mosquito. "Guess we'd better light a smudge."

The smudge was a small fire. It put off more smoke than flames. The smoke helped keep the mosquitoes away so the children could sit on the back steps without getting too many bites.

Other neighbors were sitting on their back steps, too. Some sat on their front steps or porches. In the evening, a lot of people relaxed by sitting outside where they could talk with their neighbors and passersby.

A baby's cry broke through the evening air. Polly laughed. "That reminds me of the babies in the trees at the Midsummer Festival. You didn't see them, Grant." She told him about the Swedish cradles.

"Indians sometimes hang their babies in cradles from the trees, too," Grant said.

Polly looked confused. "I thought the Indian women carried their babies on their backs."

"Sometimes they do," Grant agreed. "But the women often hang the cradles in trees or lean them against trees or tipis while they work."

Brita nodded. "That makes sense. It would be hard to work with a baby on your back."

Walter moved to a lower step beside Grant to get out of the smoke the wind blew into his face. "Did you know Brita's parents were attacked by Indians when Per was a baby, Grant?"

Grant's face was in a shadow, and Walter couldn't see him well, but he heard him grunt in surprise. "Where?"

"It was during the Sioux Uprising," Brita explained. "My mother told us all about it at the Midsummer Festival."

"Did she tell you why the Dakota fought?" Grant asked.

"They wanted the land back that they had sold to Americans." Brita tossed her braids behind her back. "That seems selfish to me."

"The Dakota, or Sioux, believe that the land belongs to everyone. *Wakan Tanka,* or the Great Spirit, only lets people use the land."

"Wakan Tanka." Polly repeated the words slowly. "Is that what the Dakota Indians call God?"

Grant nodded. "Yes. The Indians didn't know the white people believed the Indians were giving the land away forever. The Dakota didn't believe they owned the land, so how could they give it away?"

"But my parents built a farm on some land," Brita said. "Doesn't that mean they owned that land?"

Grant shrugged. "The Indians didn't believe anyone owned the land—not the white people and not the Indians. The Indians needed to hunt on the land the white people had settled."

"They didn't have to attack my parents' farm and kill my uncle."

Walter had never heard the usually cheerful Brita sound so full of anger. He understood why she was so angry, but he understood how the Indians felt about the land, too.

"When the Indians agreed to let the settlers and soldiers use their land," Grant was saying, "the government promised to see the Indians had everything they needed. They promised to give the Indians food if they couldn't find enough game to feed their people. Sometimes the promises were broken. Just before the Sioux Uprising, the Sioux in Minnesota weren't getting the food they'd been promised. When they complained, the bad white man who was in charge of the food said the Indians should eat grass. That made them very angry."

"He shouldn't have said that," Brita agreed. "Still, why

should the Indians have attacked innocent settlers? Why didn't they just attack the people who didn't keep their promises and give them food?"

"It doesn't seem like the Indians acted fairly, does it?" Grant asked. "But the white people didn't act fairly, either. Remember what happened to the Indians after the uprising?"

"We learned about that in school," Polly said. "Some were hung for murdering people. The rest of the Sioux were sent west, where there are no states."

"Yes," Grant said. "Even the Dakota who didn't fight in the uprising were sent away to live on a reservation. Even the women and children and old men who didn't fight. Even the Dakota who protected white people from being killed by the warring Dakota. Was that fair?"

Brita squirmed. "No. I guess neither side was fair. But the Indians didn't have to kill my uncle."

Walter felt like squirming inside. He didn't like the way the settlers had been treated by the Indians. He didn't like the way the Indians had been treated by the settlers, either. Did all new countries start by taking land away from the people who'd lived there first?

He was glad when Polly changed the subject and started talking about the parade.

It seemed to Walter that midnight would never come. None of the neighbors were going to bed, either. Porches and steps were filled with people, as were the street and alleyway. Voices sounded clear in the night air. Light from kerosene lamps shown in every house.

"I wish we lived in Philadelphia," he said finally.

"Why?" Polly asked.

"Philadelphia started celebrating the centennial three days ago, on July 1, and they've been celebrating ever since.

They even have a new liberty bell to ring in the country's next one hundred years."

"What do you think the United States will be like in 1976, one hundred years from now?" Grant asked. "Do you think there will even be a United States of America then? Maybe some other country will win it in a war."

The thought sent a shudder through Walter.

"I hope there will always be a United States!" Polly exclaimed.

"I saw a picture in a magazine yesterday," Walter said. "It showed what war might be like in 1976. Hot air balloons filled the sky. Soldiers were in the baskets below the balloons, shooting at each other. Some of the soldiers put boards between the baskets so they could climb into their enemies' balloons while they were in the air. Wouldn't that be something?"

They all agreed it would be.

Walter didn't have a watch, and neither did the other children. They didn't need one. They knew when it was midnight.

Small firecrackers had been going off for hours. Suddenly Roman candles and rockets and other fireworks displays filled the air with noise and the sky with brilliant color and light.

Boom!

"What was that?" Polly clapped her hands over her ears.

"Sounds like a cannon." Walter had to yell to be heard over the din.

Bells clanged and clamored. Steam whistles from nearby mills blew loud and long. Somewhere, pistols or rifles were being shot.

Polly rushed into the house. A minute later she came back

38

carrying pans and kettle lids. She handed them out to her friends. In a minute they were marching around the yard, clanging the pans and lids together and creating a wonderful noise.

People cheered and called to each other across their yards.

Walter and the others jumped up and down, hollering at the tops of their voices. Their parents came out and joined them.

Mama and Aunt Tina grabbed the girls' hands and danced around in a circle. Soon the men and boys joined in.

All too soon, the adults made the children go to bed. *It did no good,* Walter thought.

Outside his window, he could see crowds filling the streets. Their cheers and songs filled the usually quiet night. Fireworks still decorated the sky.

I'll never sleep tonight, he thought. *And the Fourth of July has just started. It's going to be a great day!*

CHAPTER 5

Independence Day

"Wake up, sleepyhead."

Walter groaned as someone shook him. He opened his eyes. His father was standing over his bed, grinning.

"I'm leaving for the railroad station now. Better get up and get ready for the parade. You might have a hard time getting through the crowded streets."

Walter whisked out of bed, wide awake now. What a day was ahead!

A short while later, Walter had to admit that his father had been right about the streets. They were so crowded with people and carriages and wagons and horses that it was hard to get through. It took a lot longer than usual to get to Hennepin and Washington Avenues, not far from the Mississippi River, where the parade started.

Since the bank was closed for the day, Uncle Enoch wasn't working. He helped the children carry the bunting for the flag. Aunt Tina carried baskets filled with the candy they'd made the night before.

"It looks like Polly was right," Walter said to Grant as they passed one of the many groups that would be in the parade. "Every group in the city will have a display in the parade. We've already passed the police and the fire department."

"All the nationalities are having displays, too," Grant said. "There's the Norwegian Harmonia Society, and the Scandia Society, and the African citizens' Jubilee Singers. Only the Indians aren't represented."

Walter darted a glance at Grant. His friend had almost sounded angry. "Lots of businesses will have displays, too."

"My father is going to be in the flour mill display." Brita's face showed how proud she was of him.

"Our flag will be the last display before the business displays," Polly told her.

Walter was impressed with the way Polly gathered all the children in the flag together. She knew where each one needed to be to make the flag work right. She helped the girls and boys fit their stars on just right. She showed Walter and Grant and the other boys holding the flag's red and white stripes where they needed to stand and how to make sure that they stayed the right distance apart.

Walter's heart raced as their turn to enter the parade neared. They watched group after group start. Many of the groups had bands playing patriotic tunes following them.

41

Walter wished their flag had such a band.

Suddenly it was their turn! The group of children giggled and darted laughing glances at each other as they began the two-mile walk.

All along the parade, the crowd cheered for the children's flag. Walter's chest swelled with pride. It was much more exciting to be in the parade than just watching it.

The crowd seemed even larger from the street. "Look, Grant," Walter called. "There're people watching us from every window on every floor of every building."

"There are even people watching from rooftops."

Many of the buildings were draped in cloth. Red, white, and blue bunting hung everywhere. Each building had at least one flag. Evergreen trees covered with miniature flags were everywhere.

"Like Christmas in July," Polly said when they saw the first one.

After their part in the parade was over and they were carrying the taffy baskets through the crowd, they heard many people say the children's flag was the best display in the parade.

Polly had been right about the candy, too. Everyone seemed hungry, and there was no place open to buy anything. The friends could see the rest of the parade while they sold their candy, and it didn't take long to finish.

"Look at all the money we made!" Polly rejoiced. "This has been a wonderful day, hasn't it? What should we do when the parade is over? There are picnics, and races, and—"

Walter didn't wait for her to finish. "Grant and I are going to try to get into the baseball game."

"The Minneapolis Blue Stockings are playing a team of professional ballplayers from Massachusetts," Grant explained.

Polly's brows met in puzzlement. "Minneapolis doesn't have a professional baseball club, does it?"

"No," both boys answered at once. "The professional team tours the country and plays teams like the Minneapolis team for fun," Walter explained.

"Billie Bohn is the hurler for the Massachusetts team." Grant laughed. "People say he can throw a curveball. As if anyone could throw a ball and make it curve in the air!"

"Our Blue Stockings will take the stuffing out of Bohn's team," Walter assured. "The Blue Stockings have won almost all their matches this year. The hurler is really good. He'll probably make all Bohn's players whiff, and strike them all out."

"What's a 'whiff'?" Brita asked.

"That means the batsman misses the ball," Walter explained. The willow, or bat, just makes a 'whiff' sound in the air."

"I've never seen a real baseball match." Polly's eyes danced. "Can Brita and I go with you?"

Walter snorted. "You don't know anything about baseball."

Grant grinned. "If you and Brita go to the match, you'll be kranklets."

Polly crossed her arms across her chest. "Grant LaPierre, are you calling us names?"

"No. Kranklets are girls who go to baseball matches. Kranks are the men who watch the matches."

"Oh." The anger slipped away from Polly's face. "Kranklet doesn't sound like a very nice word."

"I don't think I want to see a silly old baseball match anyway," Brita said. "Let's go to the picnic instead, Polly."

"I think it would be fun to do something new," Polly

protested. Then she smiled at Brita. "But picnics are fun, too. Besides, I don't want to spend any of our taffy money to get into the baseball match. See you later, boys."

There was a crowd of men and boys at the Blue Stockings' fenced ballpark on Eighth Street. Walter was glad to be there with Grant. It would be more fun with a friend. He'd liked Grant from the first day they met, but their friendship was even better because they shared a love for baseball.

The excitement among the kranks waiting for the teams to arrive at the ballpark was almost as great as it had been along the parade. Kranks on every side of them joked about Bohn's curveball.

"Guess the Massachusetts team thinks we're all stupid out here in the west," one man said.

"The Blue Stockings will show that team how to play ball," another boasted.

Suddenly the crowd broke into cheers. "Here come the Blue Stockings!"

Sure enough, the team was coming. They had on their new uniform of white flannel, with a blue shield on the chest. A blue stripe ran down the side of their pantaloons, and of course, they wore blue stockings.

Walter grabbed Grant's arm. "Look! There's the Blue Stockings' captain, Charlie Smith! He's coming right by us!"

Walter's heart beat faster than a trolley bell. He could reach right out and touch Mr. Smith. So he did. Swallowing hard, he touched the sleeve of the man's bright uniform.

"You'll beat those old Massachusetts ballplayers, Mr. Smith. You're the best pitcher there is."

The pitcher grinned down at him. "You sure know your ballplayers, boy. What's your name?"

"W—Walter, sir. Walter Fisk."

Smith nodded at Grant. "This a friend of yours?"

"Yes, sir."

"My name's Grant LaPierre, sir."

Smith dug his elbow into the side of the ballplayer standing next to him. "I think I need a boy to watch my bat during the match. How about you, Scallon?"

Walter gasped. Scallon was the club's catcher. He was rubbing his chin and looking the boys over, like he was trying to decide whether they were to be trusted with the club's most important players' bats. Walter held his breath until his chest hurt, waiting for his answer. Boys carrying the players' bats could watch the match for free.

"I could sure use a batboy," Scallon said slowly, still rubbing his chin. "I guess these two will do for us as well as any boys. But say, you two are from Minneapolis, aren't you? Wouldn't want any St. Paul boys watching my bat."

Walter could see the twinkle in the big man's eyes. He grinned. People from Minneapolis and St. Paul always teased each other and pretended their own town was the best. "I'm from Minneapolis now. I moved here from Cincinnati a few weeks ago."

Smith raised his eyebrows. "A world traveler. I'd say that makes us even more fortunate to have you help us. What about you, Grant?"

"I'm from Minneapolis, too."

"Not a world traveler like your friend here, huh?"

Grant hesitated, and Walter glanced at him. Why didn't he answer?

Finally he did. "I've never been to Cincinnati, sir. I was in Dakota Territory once, though."

Smith slapped a hand on Grant's shoulder. "Well, that's

something to brag about all right. Learn to play baseball out there?"

"No, sir."

Walter laughed as Grant's face turned red at Captain Smith's teasing. "We like to play baseball, though. One day, we hope to be as good as you two."

Smith handed his bat to Walter. "Come along then, and see how it's done."

Grant took Scallon's bat, and the boys followed the men onto the field.

When they got to the bench where the club sat, Walter glanced at Grant. A huge grin stretched across Grant's narrow face. Walter figured his own grin was just as wide. His face hurt, he was smiling so hard.

There were no bleachers for the kranks. Everyone had to stand, and there was quite a crowd for this special centennial match. It seemed to Walter that every one of the kranks was cheering for the Blue Stockings.

The Massachusetts club was up to bat first. Walter was as proud of Captain Smith as he would have been of his own father when Smith struck out the first two batsmen.

The third batsman hit the ball far into the outfield. The crowd roared for the Blue Stockings to get the ball and stop the batsman as he raced around the sandbag bases, his legs pumping.

An outfielder threw the ball to Captain Smith. Walter's throat burned from yelling so loud. He could hear the ball whiz through the air when Smith threw it to the catcher, Scallon. The ball sounded like it cracked Scallon's hands when he caught it. Walter saw him wince, but he held on tight and tagged the runner out.

The crowd went wild. That was the third out! Captain

Smith and his team had kept the professionals from scoring for the first inning.

When the clubs changed and the Blue Stockings came up to bat, Walter could see Scallon's hands were red from catching the ball. The catcher stuck his hands in the pail of drinking water. Walter was sure it was to make his hands stop hurting and swelling.

He glanced at Grant. Grant was watching Scallon, too, but only out of the corner of his eye. Walter guessed that Grant didn't want to embarrass the catcher. None of his clubmates asked about his hands.

Like all ballplayers, Scallon had a number of crooked fingers. Couldn't be a ballplayer and not have your fingers broken a few times. Some people called baseball the game of the national finger smasher.

When Smith called the club together for a minute to give the batting order, Walter whispered to Grant, "I heard that Boston's first baseman started wearing a leather glove last year when he played. Maybe it would be a good idea if all the players wore gloves."

As the Blue Stockings' first batsman walked up to home base to take his place, the crowd called out to the Massachusetts pitcher.

"Let's see that curveball, Bohn!"

"Make it take a left turn at first base, Bohn!"

Walter and Grant snickered. It wasn't nice to jeer, but a pitcher should know better than to brag he could throw a ball and make it curve.

The batsman teased the pitcher, too. "Give me a high ball, but see you make it circle all the way around me first!"

Walter knew that the pitcher was supposed to give the batsman a high ball or a low ball, whichever the batsman wanted. If the pitcher didn't put the ball where the batsman called for nine times, the batsman could walk to first base.

The batsman didn't make it to first base. The ball didn't circle around him, but he couldn't hit it, either. Not even a nick.

Whiff! Whiff! Whiff! Whiff!

Four strikes and he was out.

"That ball *does* curve," he mumbled to Smith as he walked back to the bench.

Smith snorted. "Goes against the laws of nature for a ball to curve in the air. You just can't hit the ball today and don't want to admit it."

The next player did as poorly as the first. And the next. Three batters up, and three batters out.

Walter and Grant exchanged sober glances as the Blue Stockings took the field again. The cheerful pitcher and catcher who'd invited them to be batboys had lost their smiles.

The match went from bad to worse. Not one Blue Stocking player got a hit off Bohn's curveball. Not one Blue Stocking hit a foul ball or walked to first base.

By the time the match was over, even the crowd and Blue Stocking players were grudgingly admitting Bohn threw a curveball that was unbeatable.

"As sorry as I am to lose," Smith said to Walter, "I have to admit that's the best pitching I've ever seen."

Walter admired him for admitting it.

"If you're looking for a player to copy," Smith continued, "I suggest you copy Bohn's way of pitching."

On the way home, Grant said, "I sure wish the Blue Stockings had won, especially since we were watching their bats."

"Me, too."

Warm happiness flooded Walter's chest. It was good to have a friend who liked the same things he did.

They walked on for half a block. Grant had his hands stuffed in his trouser pockets. Walter clacked a small branch along the picket fences lining the yards they passed.

Finally Walter glanced at Grant out of the corner of his eye. Grant glanced back. At the same time, they grinned.

"I sure want to learn how to throw a curveball, though," Grant said.

"Me, too."

Grant and Walter spent as much time as they could spare from chores the next day practicing pitching in Walter's backyard. When dusk came, they still hadn't thrown one curveball. Walter's arm was sore from trying.

The next morning when he went out to cut kindling for the kitchen stove, Walter couldn't resist trying to throw a curveball again. After half a dozen times, he saw Grant hurrying into the yard with a rolled up newspaper in his hands.

He tossed the ball from one hand to another and back again. "I still can't throw a curveball."

Grant didn't even bother to reply. "Have you seen the Minneapolis *Tribune* this morning?"

"The newspaper? No. Why? Does it say something about the baseball match?"

Grant shook his head hard. A lock of his black hair fell over his forehead. He pushed it away impatiently. "No. Read this headline."

He opened the paper. Walter held one side of the page and Grant the other. Walter read aloud the headline Grant pointed out.

"Brave Custer Gone. General Custer Killed."

CHAPTER 6
The Battle

"Custer killed!" Walter sat down hard on a stump beside the woodpile. A painful lump grew in his chest.

"That's not all." Grant looked grim. "All of his men were killed except one scout."

Walter read the article as fast as he could. "I can't believe this."

"It happened days ago, in June."

"When we celebrated the country's one-hundredth birthday, Custer and his men were dead, and none of us knew it." Walter felt sick to his stomach.

He read part of the article again, out loud this time. " 'General Custer found the Indian camp, about two thousand lodges, on the Little Horn, and immediately attacked the camp. Custer took five companies and charged the thickest portion of the camp.' "

Grant kicked hard at a wood chip. "Why does the cavalry attack Indian camps with women and children? Why can't they just fight warriors?"

Walter wished he had an answer, but he didn't. He read more of the article out loud. " 'Custer, his two brothers, nephew, and brother-in-law were all killed, and not one of his detachment escaped.' " Walter looked up at Grant. "Imagine losing that many in your family at one time. How awful!"

Grant nodded. "Yes."

"It says here that General Terry was on his way to meet Custer when the battle happened."

"Custer met with General Terry in St. Paul last spring to plan the campaign against the Indians. The army's headquarters in charge of forts in Minnesota, Dakota Territory, and Montana Territory is in St. Paul, you know. General Terry is in charge there."

"Have you seen him?" Walter asked.

"Yes, and Custer, too."

Walter stared at him. He wished he'd seen the famous general!

"Hey!"

Per's call startled Walter. He looked up to see Per leaning on the picket fence that divided their backyards. Per's blue eyes were blazing. "Did you hear the news? Did you hear what those murdering savages did to Custer and his men?"

"Yes." An uneasy feeling wriggled through Walter's chest.

51

The Indians won this battle, but the soldiers won others. Were the Indians any more murdering savages than the soldiers who had attacked them?

Grant propped his fists on his hips. "Custer attacked an Indian village. There were women and children there. Do you think the Indian men shouldn't have tried to protect their families?"

"The cavalry only attacks hostile Indians," Per said. "Hostile means warriors who attack settlers and soldiers."

Grant shook his head. "No it doesn't. Hostile Indians are what the government calls any Indians who aren't on their reservations."

"If they aren't on their reservations, they're breaking their treaties and deserve whatever happens to them," Per yelled.

"Their treaties say they can hunt on land outside the reservation," Grant explained in a voice as angry as Per's. "Tribes go out hunting every summer. That's all these Indians were doing probably."

Per's hands clutched around a couple fence pickets. "I wish I were old enough to join the cavalry. I'd show those redskins they can't get away with killing white men."

"Think you're a better fighter than Custer?" Grant challenged.

Walter jumped to his feet and held out one hand toward Grant and one toward Per. "You two don't have to fight about it! We can't help what the cavalry and the Indians do to each other." He turned to Grant. "The Indians killed Per's uncle, remember? I guess he has a reason to be angry with them."

Grant kicked at another wood chip. "I wish the cavalry would leave the Indians alone."

Walter shifted his feet uneasily. "It says in the article

that not much is known about the raid yet. Maybe we'll know more later."

The back door slammed. "Walter, I need more wood for the stove," his mother called.

"Have you seen the newspaper, Mama?" He crossed the yard and handed it to her.

She gasped when she read the headline. Then she scanned the article quickly. "Poor Mr. Johnson! His son was with Custer, remember? He must be among the dead. The poor, poor man."

Grant looked puzzled. "Who is Mr. Johnson?"

"A Swedish clerk at the mercantile," Per explained. "I wouldn't try telling him or his friends that Custer shouldn't have attacked the Indians. His son had a lot of friends in this neighborhood. He was a good man. He didn't deserve to die that way."

"No one does," Mama said quietly. "Wars are never good for either side. But right now, Walter has chores to do. Bring in that kindling, Walter, and fill the coal bucket."

"Yes, ma'am," he muttered, starting to pick up the wood. *You'd think a mother would understand that an Indian battle where Custer was killed was more important than chores!* he thought, but he knew better than to say it out loud.

Every day there was a new report in the newspaper about the battle between Custer and the Indians. Since only one of Custer's men survived, people weren't sure what was and wasn't true about the battle. Walter could tell that a lot of things were just rumor.

Walter, Grant, Polly, and Brita started meeting each morning to read the latest reports on Custer. After that they'd read the new story by Mark Twain about Tom Sawyer. The newspaper was printing part of it each day. Some days they could hardly wait to find out what happened next, but they *had* to wait!

"It's funny to think of Tom Sawyer playing on the same Mississippi River that we live near, isn't it?" Walter asked Grant one day after they'd read the latest serial.

Grant grinned. "Yes. I don't think our parents would like it if we had many adventures like his, though."

Walter laughed. "You're right."

"Would you like me to show you some of my favorite places along the river?"

"Sure!"

Along the way, they passed by the river area Walter had already come to know. Flour mills, like the one where Brita and Per's father worked, stood many stories tall beside the river. Lumber mills filled the air with a pine smell Walter loved. Sometimes the river was so full of pine logs he could hardly see the water. The trees were cut and trimmed in the forests of northern Minnesota and Wisconsin, and then they floated for many miles down the river to the sawmills.

"Father says before long logs won't be floated down the river anymore," he told Grant. "The railroads will carry the logs faster and safer. Can't have any logjams on a railroad car."

He liked the deafening roar of St. Anthony Falls. The huge waterfalls was said to be the largest in the country except Niagara Falls.

"The Sioux Indians used to camp along the river near St. Anthony Falls," Grant told him. "But white people wanted to use the falls for power to run their mills, and the towns of St. Anthony and Minneapolis grew up around the mills. Now St. Anthony and Minneapolis are one town, and the Indians are gone."

"Did the Indians use the falls for power, too?"

"They thought the falls had a different kind of power. The area around the falls was considered holy land by many Indian nations. The Sioux called the falls *Minnerara.*"

Walter repeated the word so he would remember it. "What does that mean?"

"Curling water." Grant pointed at a tree-covered island below the falls. "That's Spirit Island."

"Did the Indians give it that name?"

"Yes. The name came from a story about an Indian woman, *Ampato Sapa.* Her name means Dark Day in English. She loved her Indian brave husband very much. Sometimes Indian men had more than one wife. When Dark Day's husband took a second wife, Dark Day was very sad. She put her baby in a canoe and paddled over the falls. Dark Day and her baby were both killed. See the spray of water where the water from the falls hits the end of the island?"

"Yes."

"The Indians believe Dark Day's spirit is in that spray."

"That's a sad story," Walter said.

"Some of the Christian stories are sad, too."

"Yes, but Jesus came to take away the sadness and give people joy and hope."

"Christian Indians are punished unfairly by white people, just like Indians who aren't Christian," Grant said, picking his way along a narrow path beside the river.

Walter stopped, surprised. "Aren't you a Christian, Grant?"

Grant hesitated. "I know the stories about Jesus. I know He's God's Son and loved people so much that He came to earth so we could learn about Him, and live with Him and God in heaven when we die. What I don't understand is why white people who are Christians are so mean to Christian Indians."

"I don't understand, either," Walter said slowly. "I don't believe God wants Christians to treat each other that way, or to treat anyone else unkindly."

Soon Walter and Grant stopped talking and gave their attention to following the path that wound through the trees and brush close to the brown water.

Walter liked watching the many boats that made the river seem more crowded than a business street. Flatboats and barges were piled with wooden barrels and crates filled with merchandise for trade and business. Steamboats with their paddle wheels and beautiful decks carried passengers. He used to watch them on the river that flowed through Cincinnati, too, and the sight of them made him homesick. His father said before many years passed, there wouldn't be steamboats anymore. They wouldn't be needed when a person could go anywhere in the country on a railroad, and go there faster.

Soon they reached an area where there were no mills and the town couldn't be seen. The banks of the river were wild. Berries and wild plum trees grew along with the other trees and bushes. The sounds of insects and frogs and birds were loud without the town noises in the background.

"Let's pretend we're Indian boys," Grant said.

"All right. What do we do?"

"Pretend we're hunting. Sioux boys hunt small animals with their bows and arrows by the time they are five years old. By the time he is our age, a Sioux boy has hunted his first buffalo calf."

"That sounds a lot more fun than going to school!"

"Learning to hunt is as important as school to an Indian

boy. If he doesn't learn to hunt, he won't be able to get meat to feed his family when he's a man."

"I never thought of it that way."

"Indian boys have to learn to be very patient. Sometimes they have to sit very still and quiet for a long time. That's so the animals and birds get used to them sitting there and aren't afraid to come close. They have to learn to watch for signs of game, too. They need to know how to tell whether an animal track in the mud or snow was made by a squirrel, or a rabbit, or a deer, or a wolf."

"I know what squirrel and rabbit tracks look like. I've seen them in snow in our yard."

Grant nodded. "Me, too. There are other things to learn. Look over here."

He pointed to an area of wild grass beneath a bush.

Walter frowned. "What am I looking at?"

"See how the grass here isn't as springy as the grass around it?"

Walter looked closer. "It's pushed down a little, in a circle or oval shape."

"A deer slept here. Probably last night."

Walter's mouth dropped open. "How do you know that?"

"My father taught me. He used to trap animals when he was young. My grandfather was a trapper, too. He taught my father all about the ways of animals."

"I wish *my* father could teach *me* things like that."

An hour later Walter leaned back beside Grant against the riverbank with a contented sigh. Trees hanging over the river's edge shaded him from the July sun. The ground among the weeds that grew along the bank was cool and moist, and the breeze off the river felt good.

"Pretending we were hunters was fun," Walter said. "I

wish we had rifles or bows and arrows so we could really hunt."

"Maybe we can make slingshots. We could hunt small things with them."

"I think it would have been fun to be an Indian. Where did you learn so much about Indians, anyway?"

It was a minute before Grant answered. "From my grandfather and father. Trappers and Indians were often friends. When my grandfather came to this area, Minnesota wasn't a state yet."

"Were there many white people here then?"

"A few. Some soldiers and trappers. There were some missionaries who stayed with the Indians on one of the lakes near here. Later the missionaries translated the Bible into the Sioux language."

"That must have taken a long time. The Bible is so big. I can't imagine even reading the whole thing, and they translated all of it into another language."

Walter paused. "If your grandfather and father knew a lot of Indians, did they have friends who were Indians?"

Grant picked up a twig and twirled it between his hands. "Yes. They had many Indian friends."

"Does your father have Indian friends who were sent to reservations?"

"Many."

Walter tried to think what it would be like to have a friend you liked, maybe a good friend like Grant, sent away. It would be different than moving from Cincinnati to Minneapolis because of your father's work.

A thought struck him suddenly. "Are any of your father's friends with the Indians the cavalry is fighting?"

Grant tossed the twig into the river and watched the

water carry it downstream. "Probably. The Sioux sent away from Minnesota went to a reservation in Nebraska Territory, but many of them hunt outside the reservations during the summer, as treaties say they can do."

"Your father has friends on the Indian side of the battles and our neighbors have friends in the cavalry, like Mr. Johnson's son who was killed with Custer. That seems strange, doesn't it?"

"Yes." Grant cleared his throat. "Why did you try to stick up for the Indians when Per called them names?"

Walter shrugged. "I guess for the same reason you stick up for them. I think everyone should be treated fairly. And I think there are Indians who are good and Indians who are bad, the same as some white people are good and some aren't."

"Most people talk like Indians are no better than insects that need to be killed."

"Maybe that's because they're afraid. They remember that Indians have attacked white settlers. Maybe the Indians are afraid, too."

Grant nodded. "Afraid of losing their land and their way of life. Afraid white people will kill their children."

"My uncle Tim is a lawyer in Cincinnati. He's an abolitionist and believes slavery is wrong. He told me how Indians helped slaves escape to Canada before the war. I guess I've always thought most Indians were good people. They just live differently than we do."

"I think I'd like your uncle Tim. Slavery is a bad thing."

"When Polly's mother was a girl, she helped a slave escape."

Grant sat up and stared at him. "Truly? That took a lot of courage. It was a dangerous thing to do. I'm going to ask her to tell me about it sometime."

Walter pushed himself up. "I suppose we'd better be getting home. Mother will have more chores for me to do. Maybe she won't be so upset with me if I bring her some berries."

He took his kerchief from his back pocket and filled it with berries. Then he tied the ends of the kerchief together so he could carry the berries home without dropping or smashing them.

He looked out across the wide Mississippi before turning toward home. He liked the quiet and beauty of the area. If he didn't know better, he wouldn't guess there was a city nearby. *I think I would have liked to be an Indian,* he thought, *before the white people came.*

Life on their street wasn't quiet and peaceful like the riverside. Today it was less quiet and peaceful than usual.

"Look, Grant," Walter said as they neared their homes. "I think someone is moving into Per and Brita's house!"

CHAPTER 7
Grasshopper Plague

Per was taking a trunk out of the back of a wagon. A blond-haired boy about Walter's age was helping him. A woman was talking with Mrs. Swenson. Even from where he was standing, Walter could hear the woman's Swedish accent. It was even stronger than Mrs. Swenson's accent. Two children—a girl about six and a boy who looked a year or two younger—stood close by the women.

The Swenson's front door slammed, and Brita raced down the walk to the wagon. Seeing Walter and Grant, she waved eagerly. "Hello! My cousins are moving in with us!" A moment later she turned her attention to the young girl.

"I'd better get home," Grant said. "You can tell me about Brita's cousins later."

Walter hurried inside. He found his mother and Judith in the kitchen. He set his handkerchief of berries on the wooden worktable and fanned a hand in front of his face. "Whew! Is it hot in here. I forgot you baked bread this morning. It sure smells good, though." The smell of fresh baked bread always made his mouth water.

Mama's glance darted to the kerchief. "Walter Fisk, whatever have you in that kerchief?"

"Berries. I—I found them growing wild, and thought you'd like some." He was always in trouble when she called him by his whole name!

She shook her head. "It was thoughtful of you to bring the berries, but I'll never get those stains out of your kerchief, even with boiling it." Her sigh was so large it lifted the apron that covered the entire front of her work dress. "I guess I should be glad you carried them in your kerchief and not in your trouser pockets."

She untied the kerchief and tasted one of the berries. "Oh, these are wonderful!"

Judith abandoned the kerosene chimneys she was washing and grabbed some berries herself. "Yum!"

Mama grabbed her hand. "Don't eat them until you've cleaned that soot off your hands, Judith."

"Did you see the people moving in next door, Mama?" Walter asked.

"Yes. They are the Larsons, and they will be staying for a few months, but that's all I know."

"Brita said they are her cousins."

"I'm going to take a loaf of bread over later to welcome them to the neighborhood," Mama said, putting the berries in a china bowl. "Mrs. Swenson will be able to use it with all those people." She glanced down at the bowl. "Were there more berries where you found these, Walter? Enough for a pie or two?"

"Yes."

"It would be nice to make a pie for Mrs. Swenson, too. Would you mind going back and picking more berries later today? I can bake the pie first thing tomorrow morning, before the day gets too warm."

Walter grinned. Imagine his mother sending him back to the riverside! "Sure, there's lots of berries." *Now that's the kind of chore I like,* he thought.

"Can I pick berries, too, Mama?"

Walter bit back a groan. He didn't want his little sister to know where the berries grew. That was his place and Grant's, a special place where no one else could bother them. A boy needed a private place to think sometimes.

"Not today, Judith. You've dillydallied with those kerosene lamps all morning, and you still aren't done with them."

Judith wrinkled her freckled nose. "I hate cleaning kerosene lamps. Why can't we have gas lamps, like the Stevensons?"

"One day we will," her mother promised. "Walter, will you take this pan over to the Stevensons on your way to pick berries? I borrowed it the other day."

"Sure." He grabbed a tin pail from the pantry for the berries and picked up the pan his mother wanted returned. At the back door, he couldn't resist turning around and teasing Judith:

"Judith had a little lamp
   'Twas filled with kerosene.
Judith down the chimney blew
   And vanished from the scene."

Judith's face became a miniature storm cloud. "Mo-o-o-ther! Make him stop that!"

Chuckling, Walter darted down the back steps, the pail and pan clanging together. That verse always put Judith in a dither.

Of course, with the safety kerosene lamps they had in their house, there wasn't any chance Judith would blow herself up with any of them. You didn't have to blow down the chimney to extinguish the wick, like you did with the old-fashioned lamps. Even if the lamps were knocked over, they didn't explode like the old ones could.

Sometimes I think it would be fun to live like the Indians, and other times I think this modern living is great.

The next morning when the pies were out of the oven, Mama invited Judith and Walter to join her in a visit to the Swensons and Larsons. Walter was glad to have a chance to find out about their new neighbors without going over by himself.

When they arrived, Polly and Aunt Tina and Abe were already there. The women were in the kitchen having coffee and talking. After being introduced to Mrs. Larson, Walter and Judith joined the other children in the backyard.

Brita quickly introduced everyone. "This is Lars," she said, pointing to the blond-haired boy Walter had seen helping Per with the trunk the day before. "He's ten."

Walter nodded to Lars. "Hi."

"Kirstin is six, and Alex is four," Brita finished.

The younger children smiled shyly at Walter and Judith. Walter smiled back. "Hi! Welcome to Minneapolis."

Judith hurried over to where Kirstin, Abe, and Alex were playing beneath a large maple tree.

Walter sat down on the wooden steps where Polly, Brita, and Lars were visiting. He was surprised to see that Lars, Kirstin, and Alex's clothes looked worn and patched.

Walter wished he weren't so shy about meeting new

children. After a couple minutes of listening to Polly and Brita chatter, he wondered if maybe Lars wasn't a little shy, too. At least now he wasn't the new kid on the block. Lars was the new kid.

Walter took a deep breath. "My sister and I live next door," he said to Lars. "I'm ten, too. It will be good to have another boy next door."

Lars smiled. "Yah."

He didn't say much back. What can I say next? Walter wondered. "Um, did you just arrive from Sweden?"

"We are from Sweden, yah." Lars bobbed his head. "We come from Sweden three years ago."

He spoke slowly, and Walter wondered if he didn't know English very well yet. Like many of the Swedish people in the neighborhood, he said "w's" like "v's" and "th's" like "t's".

"Where have you been living since then?"

"On a farm. We are homesteaders. We live over one hundred miles away, on the Minnesota River."

So that's why Lars's skin was so much darker than most Swedes in the city. Living on a farm, he must have had to help in the fields and been out in the sun a lot. "If you have a farm, why are you staying here?"

Lars's blond brows met above his eyes as he concentrated on Walter's words. "What you say?"

Walter repeated his question. This time Lars understood.

"*Far* sent us here. Grasshoppers came and ate all our crop, so there isn't enough food to feed all of our family."

"Aren't there towns near your farm where you can buy food?" Walter asked.

"There are towns, but the grasshoppers ate all the gardens there, too. The railroads don't come to the towns yet, so it is hard to get food there."

Walter nodded. "My father is a railroad engineer. He told me that the railroad companies aren't building out west because the grasshoppers are keeping new settlers away from that part of the country."

"Yah, the grasshoppers have come every summer. Farmers are very poor because the grasshoppers eat our crops. Many farmers have left Minnesota. Wagon trains of farmers left our part of Minnesota this summer. Some are going to Oregon to find new land. Some are going to the Black Hills."

"The Black Hills? But the Black Hills are on Indian land. White settlers aren't supposed to go there."

Lars lifted the shoulders of his thin shirt in a shrug. "People are poor, and there is gold in the Black Hills." His grin flashed in his tan face. "My older brother, Ole, is four-teen. He thinks *we* should go to the Black Hills and get rich."

"But the Indian treaty says white people won't go on the Indians' land," Walter protested.

Polly cleared her throat with a sound like Walter's mother made when she was upset with him in public and didn't want to make a scene. He glanced at her, and she scowled back at him.

I guess she's upset because I'm criticizing him, Walter thought.

Polly leaned forward, wrapping her arms around her skirt-covered knees. "What was it like when the grasshoppers came, Lars?"

"The grasshoppers were so thick, they filled the air, like snow in a snowstorm. We could hardly see the barn from our house. When they landed, they ate everything. The crunching noise when they ate was loud, like thunder, but a different sound, and it went on for a long time. They ate the crops in the fields and gardens, they ate the leaves and bark off the trees *Far* planted, they ate grass off the house, and—"

"Did you say they ate the grass off the *house?*" Walter asked.

"Yah. We live in a sod house. Our barn is sod, too. The grasshoppers ate the hay we had stored in the barn for our cow and oxen. The grasshoppers even came in the house and chewed on curtains and bedding. *Mor* was very mad at them for that. There was not even a blade of grass left for fifteen miles."

"It must have been awful!" Polly's eyes were huge as she listened to Lars.

Walter thought his own face must show just as much shock. It was like listening to a story of little monsters. "I've heard it's hard to kill them."

"Yah. Each one isn't hard to kill, but there are so many. When they landed, we watched through the windows. The whole earth, even the barn where they were crawling, seemed to be moving."

The younger children had moved closer to hear Lars tell about the grasshoppers. "It was scary," Kirstin said. "I cried."

"Me, too," said Alex.

"There isn't food for all of us for the winter," Lars said, "It will be hard to buy wood for heat and cooking, too. We can't use twisted hay for the stove since the grasshoppers came. So *Far* sent us to stay here. Most farmers aren't as lucky as we are. They don't have families to stay with like this, and many cannot afford to leave with the wagon trains. Their families will be cold and hungry this winter."

Walter had seen how many immigrant families in the area lived together. It was cheaper to live that way. He knew it cost a lot of money to bring a family across the ocean and start a new life.

"At church, the pastor told us how people need help because of the grasshoppers," Polly said. "The church is collecting donations of clothes and money and canned goods for the people. My mother and Walter's mother and Brita's mother are making a quilt to send." She smiled at Brita. "Brita and I are helping with the quilt. It's fun."

"Are you going to send the bunting we used for the flag in the parade?" Walter asked.

"That's a wonderful idea!" Polly's face lit up. "I don't think we need it for the quilt, but we could make blankets or clothing for babies."

"Or send the material and let the mothers make what they need for their children," Brita suggested.

"You'd have to send thread, too," Lars told them. "Many grasshopper sufferers can't even afford thread."

"Papa said the railroads are carrying donations to the grasshopper counties free," Walter said. "That's the way the railroad companies are helping." It left a warm feeling in his chest, knowing his father and the company he worked for were helping the farmers out.

"What is the parade flag you used the bunting for?" Lars asked.

Polly told him about the children's flag for the Fourth of July parade.

"Did the towns near you celebrate the centennial on the Fourth of July?" Walter asked.

Lars nodded. "Yah. People could take rides in a hot air balloon, and there were horse races and a parade. *Mor* took Kirstin and Alex to see the parade."

"Didn't you want to see it?"

"Yah, I wanted to see it, but older brother, Ole, and I had to work in the fields. Only a few grasshoppers had come then, and we hoped we would still have crops to harvest this fall. Ole and I go to school in the evenings, when the work in the field is done. If we went to the parade, we would have had to work instead of go to school. I would have liked to see the parade, though."

Polly looked as surprised at Lars's story as Walter felt. "I think it's terrible you didn't get to see it," she said.

Walter thought so, too, but he didn't say so. He didn't like to have people feel sorry for him, and he thought Lars wouldn't like it, either. "Sometimes a man has to do what is right instead of what is fun."

"Yah." Lars gave him a grateful smile that made Walter glad he'd defended him.

But when he walked home, Walter couldn't help worrying about the country that had just celebrated its hundredth birthday so cheerfully.

The Indians were killing soldiers and white settlers, and the soldiers were killing Indians. Miners in the Black Hills gold rush were ignoring Indian treaties and going onto Indian land in hopes of getting rich. Grasshoppers were destroying farmers' crops and making farmers poor.

At school and church, they'd been told God loved America and its people and blessed the country because most of its people were Christians who loved God and served Him. If that was true, why did so many things seem to be going wrong in the United States?

Would there be a United States one hundred years from now? he wondered.

CHAPTER 8

A New School

With heavy hearts, Walter and Grant continued watching the newspaper for news about the Indian wars in Dakota and Montana Territories. People across the country were angry at what they called the massacre of Custer and his men. They were demanding the president and cavalry capture and punish the Sioux and Cheyenne, whether they'd been involved in the battle or not.

Finally one day Walter and Grant read that President Ulysses Grant had chosen a group of men to help Congress make an agreement between the Indians and the United States that would keep the Indians from fighting.

"Some of these men have been good friends of the

Indians," Grant told Walter. "Have you heard of this man?"

Walter read the name Grant pointed to. "Bishop Whipple." He shook his head. "Who is he?"

"He has spent many years telling the Sioux about Christ. Remember when the Sioux were punished for the Sioux Uprising, the war where Brita and Per's uncle was killed?"

"Yes. Thirty-eight Sioux warriors were hung, and most other Sioux were sent out of state to a reservation."

"That's right. At first, three hundred warriors were to be hung, but Bishop Whipple wrote President Lincoln and said that wasn't right. He told the president men shouldn't be hung as criminals for fighting for their people in a war. The president agreed with him and pardoned most of the warriors."

"He must have been a wise man to get President Lincoln to listen to him."

"The Sioux listened to Bishop Whipple, too. After the Sioux were gathered together by the soldiers and waiting to see what would happen to them, Bishop Whipple went to the Sioux and told them about Jesus. Many of the Indians became Christians."

Walter was glad to hear of a Christian white man who cared about what happened to the Indians, the way Walter thought Jesus would want.

"Maybe Bishop Whipple will help find a way for the Indians to keep hunting on the land they haven't sold to the United States yet," he said.

"I hope so."

Walter didn't think Grant looked like he had much hope. He couldn't blame him. There had been another battle between the Indians and the cavalry. This time the cavalry won. After the battle at Bonnet Creek, one thousand Cheyenne were sent to the Red Cloud Indian Agency.

When summer was over and it was time for the school year to begin, Walter and Grant still didn't know what kind of agreement the men and Congress had decided to offer the Indians.

"This is a big school!" Lars stared up at the front of the two-story brick building. "The school we went to by the farm is made of logs, and there is only one room."

Grant laughed. "Minneapolis needs large schools. There's over thirty-eight thousand people in this city now."

Walter just shook his head. "Minneapolis isn't a large city next to Cincinnati."

Walter dodged the elbow Grant tried to poke into his ribs. "You're always talking about how much better Cincinnati is, but that city is a lot older. Minneapolis is on the edge of the frontier, and growing fast. There were only about forty-five hundred people here ten years ago."

Walter was glad he and Grant were in the same class. He hadn't told his friend, but he was nervous about starting school. He still didn't know many boys their age.

Lars wasn't in their class. His English wasn't good enough for him to study with most of the boys their age, even though Walter knew Lars was smart.

The classroom was filled with desks, each made for two students. Walter hoped to sit beside Grant, but the teacher, Miss Lee, assigned seats. Walter's last name of Fisk wasn't close to Grant's last name of LaPierre, and they ended up sitting a row apart.

Walter sat down and slid his black slate with its wooden border and his wooden pencil box on the shelf beneath his bench seat. *At least I'm not sharing my desk with a girl, like Grant is,* Walter thought.

The boy beside him had long dark hair and green eyes.

72

His name was Robert French. When Miss Lee told Robert where he was to sit, Walter smiled at him.

Robert didn't smile back. Instead he looked Walter over with a sober face. Walter felt like an animal in a cage at the zoo.

"New here, aren't you?" Robert asked in a low voice as Miss Lee continued assigning students.

"Yes. I'm from Cincinnati."

Robert crossed his arms, leaned back, and sneered. "Think you're some kind of big shot, coming from one of the biggest cities in the country?"

"No!" Walter's chest tightened with anger from the insult. *Maybe I would rather have sat beside a girl after all,* he thought.

When everyone had been assigned a seat, Miss Lee led the class in a short prayer, the same way the teacher in Cincinnati had started each school day, Walter remembered. He glanced at Robert's unfriendly face beside him and felt a sharp pang of loneliness in his chest for his old friends in Ohio.

"Walter Fisk and Robert French, will you help me hand out books?" Miss Lee asked with a smile.

Miss Lee was tall and slender, with a narrow face and pointed chin. She wore her brown hair up in a bun. Round wire glasses sat on her straight nose. She had a pleasant smile. Walking up to the front of the room to help with the books, Walter decided he would like his teacher this year.

"I understand you are new to our school this year, Walter," she said as he reached for a stack of books.

"Yes, Miss Lee."

"Perhaps one day you'll tell the class all about the city from which you came."

"Uh, yes, Miss Lee, if you want me to." Inside he groaned. After the way Robert acted about his being from Cincinnati, he wanted to fit into the class and not be noticed as different.

"Be very careful with your books," Miss Lee was saying as Walter finished passing out the books, sat down, and opened his copy of *Monroe's Fifth Reader*. "These books will be passed on to another class next year. Write your name inside the front cover. If you damage the books, you will have to pay for them."

Walter took a pencil from his pencil box and wrote his name as neatly as he could.

"You should all be good readers by now," Miss Lee said, "or you wouldn't be in fifth grade. This year we are going to teach you to speak in front of people, so we will be reading aloud from the readers every day."

Robert groaned out loud and slumped against the back of his seat.

The teacher pinned him with a sharp look. "If you are going to be speakers, one of the first things you must learn is how to breathe properly. There can be no slouching, whether you are seated or standing."

Robert's face grew red. Walter bit his lips to keep from chuckling.

"Now," she continued, "let's all practice. Sit up straight. Don't let your backs touch the backs of the benches. Good! Now take a deep breath. Hold it. Hold it. Hold it."

Walter's face felt as if it would explode if she didn't stop saying hold it.

"Let your breath out slowly."

Walter let it out, but not slowly.

"Speakers need to be able to control their breathing well. Let's try again."

Walter thought it was the strangest reading class he'd ever been in.

They'd received their geography books after the reading class was over. Miss Lee talked about the new state, Colorado.

Finally a bell rang, and the students were allowed to go outside for lunch. Walter and Grant found a spot in the shade of a large elm and opened their small tin lunch pails. They looked for Lars but didn't see him.

"There's a friend I haven't seen all summer," Grant said, pointing at a group of boys across the yard. "I'm going to say hello to him. Be back in a few minutes."

Walter leaned back against the tree, glancing around the school ground curiously while he bit into a crisp apple. A breeze tossed the leaves in the branches above him. The yard was alive with children eating, playing, laughing, and talking. As usual, some boys were playing cavalry and Indians.

Another group of boys was playing marbles. Walter wondered whether that's what his friends in Cincinnati were doing now. They used to play marbles a lot on their lunch hours, and he'd been pretty good at it.

"Hey, Fisk, what you got for lunch?"

Before Walter could stop him, Robert grabbed his lunch pail by the thin tin handle. Walter jumped up and lunged for it. Robert easily swung the pail out of his reach.

Two boys stepped up beside Robert and glared at Walter. Walter could feel his face growing hot as he stared at the three boys. They didn't have to tell him that they were friends and would stand by each other against him.

Robert smirked and took a piece of apple cake out of the pail. "This looks good." He took a big bite out of it.

Walter balled his hands into fists at his sides, getting angrier every second.

Robert dropped the cake on the ground and stepped on it. "Wasn't good after all. Guess moms don't learn how to bake very well in Cincinnati."

Anger surged through Walter. He took a step closer. "Why, you—"

Grant stepped in front of him and calmly held out his hand toward Robert for the pail. "If you don't like his lunch, I guess you won't be needing that."

Robert scowled, but let him take the pail. "Get out of the way, Grant. Our fight isn't with you."

"Walter is my friend. We stick together." He nodded toward the two boys with Robert. "Just like you and your friends stick together. If you fight one of us, you'll have to fight us both."

Walter couldn't believe how quietly Grant spoke. He didn't sound like he was ready to fight!

Robert looked past Grant to Walter. His eyes sparked with anger. "Afraid to fight your own battles, Fisk?"

"No. Are you?"

Robert pointed a finger so close to Walter's face that he was afraid he'd go cross-eyed looking at it. He almost took a step back, but he didn't want to appear less brave than Grant.

"I'll catch you another time, scaredy-cat Fisk," Robert threatened, "when you're alone and have to fight for yourself."

He turned on his heel and stalked toward the steps leading into the school. His two friends followed.

Walter suddenly noticed a large group of boys standing about watching them. There was none of the noise of play that had filled the schoolyard earlier. Most of the children in his class had seen Robert bully him!

The group standing about parted to let them through as he and Grant walked back to the school. "I wish I were invisible," he muttered to Grant.

"You don't have anything to be embarrassed about. The stupid thing would have been to let the three of them bully you into fighting."

"All those children watching probably think I'm a scaredy-cat, like Robert said."

"They can count, can't they? When it's three against one, fighting isn't smart, and all of them know it. Look what happened to Custer when he and his men were outnumbered."

He sure has a way of making me feel better, Walter thought, glad he'd found such a good friend in Minneapolis.

"Besides," Grant said, "I should have warned you about Robert and his followers. They try to pick fights with all the new boys in school. They want to find out if any of the new students are tougher than they are. I suppose they'll pick on Lars, too, when they find out about him."

"We'd better tell him to watch out for them." *I'll be watching out for them myself,* Walter thought. "I don't really want to go back inside and sit next to Robert in class all afternoon."

Grant grinned. "Just smile at him and act like you two are best friends. It'll make him nervous."

They entered the school together, laughing.

CHAPTER 9

Bank Robbers

"Wow! Look at this, Grant!" Walter pointed to the newspaper headline.

" 'Jesse James's Gang Raids Northfield Bank!' " Grant grabbed the paper. "I don't believe it! Northfield is only about thirty miles south of here."

"I keep hearing Minneapolis is at the edge of the wild frontier," Walter said with a grin, "but I didn't think the edge was that close."

"Did you say Jesse James's gang?" Polly's voice was almost a squeak.

Walter looked across the parlor at her. Her green eyes were big and filled with fear. Her face looked white. "What's the matter?"

"Jesse James robs banks and kills people. What if he robs the bank where Papa works?"

Walter shifted his feet uncomfortably. "I don't think he'd rob a bank in a town as big as Minneapolis. It would be too dangerous."

Grant was still reading the article. "It says here that Jesse James killed a cashier at the Northfield bank because he wouldn't open the safe."

Polly gasped and looked more frightened than ever.

Grant glanced at her. "Don't worry, Polly. The towns-people shot at the gang. They killed a couple of them and wounded most of the others."

"Did they get away?" she asked breathlessly.

Grant glanced at Walter, then back at Polly. "Yes," he admitted.

Polly swallowed hard. "If the bank clerk wouldn't open the safe for them, they must not have stolen any money. Maybe they will come here next. A big town like Minneapolis would have lots more money in their banks than a little town like Northfield, wouldn't it?"

"The men are wounded," Walter reminded her. "They'll have to get their wounds bound up and heal a bit before they can do any more robbing."

"Yes," Grant agreed. "While they are holed up, every lawman in Minnesota will be looking for them or guarding their own towns especially well."

"I hope so," Polly whispered.

Walter hoped so, too. "We'd better get to school." Maybe classes would take Polly's mind off the famous outlaw.

But Jesse James and the Northfield raid were all the children at school wanted to talk about that day. At noon, boys played bank robbers instead of cavalry and Indians. Walter wished they wouldn't. Polly stood beside the schoolhouse, rubbing her arms and watching them play bank robbers with scared eyes.

When he got to his desk after lunch, Robert was grinning ear to ear. His smile sent a warning shiver down Walter's back. Robert hadn't been nice once to him since the first day of school earlier that week.

Miss Lee rapped a pointer stick on her desk. "Attention class. It's time to settle down. We're going to practice our articulation now."

Groans rose from every area of the class. Walter groaned, too. He didn't like this part of class.

"Repeat after me," Miss Lee said. "Ee-ah-oo."

"Ee-ah-oo," the class repeated faithfully.

"Ah-oo-ee," Miss Lee said next.

"Ah-oo-ee," the class repeated.

Walter had to bite his lips to keep from laughing. Everyone looked so funny!

He was glad when the articulation was over. Then Miss Lee asked him to stand at the front of the class beside her desk and read from *Monroe's Fifth Reader.*

Why does she always pick on me? he wondered, as he made his way to the front.

"We're going to practice slides today, class." Miss Lee smiled at him. "Do you know what slides are, Walter?"

"No, ma'am."

"Speakers use slides to keep their listeners' attention. It makes a speech more interesting if words aren't all spoken in the same tone. If a speech uses a word like 'up,' the speaker makes his voice slide a little higher." Miss Lee took his reader and began turning pages. "Let's turn to today's lesson, and you can try it for the class, Walter."

Suddenly she stopped turning pages, but she didn't hand him back the book. Her jaw dropped, and she looked at him in surprise.

"What is it, Miss Lee?"

"Why, today's lesson pages are covered in fresh ink."

"What?" Walter grabbed the book. Just as she'd said, the fresh ink covered most of the two pages. Walter's heart started racing. Now he'd have to pay for the book. What would his father say when he heard?

"How did this happen, Walter?"

Walter gulped so loud he thought the whole class could hear it. "I–I don't know, Miss Lee." *But I do know,* he thought. *Robert must have done this during lunch break.* "I didn't do it."

"We'll discuss this after class, Walter. Take your seat."

Walter glared at Robert all the way back to his desk. Robert grinned back at him.

"We'll *all* practice sliding, class," Miss Lee said. "Repeat after me. 'Rouse thee up!' " On the word up, she lifted her hand with the palm toward the ceiling. Her voice went from a normal pitch to a high pitch.

The class giggled but repeated the phrase, making their voices go from low to high as Miss Lee had done. When they had repeated it, everyone burst out laughing at how funny they sounded.

Everyone except Walter. He barely heard them. He was staring at the inkwell in the middle of the desk he shared with Robert. He knew Robert was still trying to make him angry enough to fight with him. He'd been avoiding Robert and his friends during recess, lunch, and before and after school all week. He didn't want to fight.

Maybe this is how the Indians feel about the cavalry, he thought, *like they are being forced to fight whether they want to or not.*

After school, Walter's stomach felt like it was filled with jumping grasshoppers as he watched all the other children leave the class. What would Miss Lee say?

He saw Robert turn around at the door and laugh at him before leaving. Grant came by his desk and bumped his fist lightly against Walter's shoulder, which made Walter feel a little bit better.

When the last classmate left the room, Walter took a deep breath and walked up to Miss Lee's desk. It was hard to wait patiently while she washed off the slate board.

When she turned around, she clasped her hands in front of him and shook her head. "Walter, you know the punishment for ruining a textbook, don't you?"

"Yes, Miss Lee. I have to pay for it so the school can buy a new one for a student next year."

"That's right. I'll have to send a note home to your parents explaining what happened."

Walter nodded, feeling miserable.

"I won't give you any other punishment this time, Walter. I am very disappointed in you, though."

Walter felt a sharp pain in his chest at the disapproval in her voice. He'd liked her from the first. She was a kind teacher. He didn't want her to think badly of him. "I didn't make that ink blot, Miss Lee," he blurted out.

"Then who did?"

"I–I think I know, but I can't prove it, so I'd best not say who I think it is."

She laid a hand on his shoulder. "You can prove to me that you didn't do this by not breaking any of the other class rules."

The pain in Walter's chest eased a bit. She was giving him another chance! She didn't think he was terrible after all.

"Mind, you will still have to pay for the book, and I will still have to send the note to your parents."

"Yes, Miss Lee." He wouldn't like showing his father the note, and asking for the money for the book, but at least Miss Lee wouldn't think he was a bad student for the rest of the year.

He didn't see any other students as he hurried down the hallway. Everyone usually left school as soon as possible after classes, but he'd hoped Grant would wait and walk home with him. His footsteps sounded loud on the stairway.

Grant wasn't on the front steps or in the schoolyard, either. Walter tried to push away the disappointment he felt as he started around the building.

"Oof!"

Walter stopped in his tracks. Where had that grunt come from?

"Oof!"

It sounded like it came from around the corner of the building. He hurried that way. When he rounded the corner, what he saw made him stop again—but only for a second. There was Grant being pummeled by Robert and one of his friends!

Anger roared through Walter like the Mississippi River over St. Anthony Falls. He dropped his lunch pail and books and lunged toward Robert. He caught him from the back around the shoulders and yanked. They hit the ground together with a thud.

"Hey!" Robert cried out in surprise. Then he twisted

around and saw who had attacked him. His fists began swinging. So did Walter's.

Walter wasn't sure whether he was winning or losing. He felt a few smart blows on his face and tried to give back as good as he got. He could tell Grant was still fighting the other guy.

They fought until all four of them lay panting on the ground. *Like hounds after a run on a hot day,* Walter thought, but he was too tired to laugh.

"How about if we call this a draw?" Robert's friend asked.

Robert scowled and drew the back of his hand across his mouth. "A draw?"

Grant sat up and held out a hand toward Robert's friend. "I'll call it a draw if you will." The other boy shook his hand, then flopped back on the grass, still panting.

Walter shrugged. "I guess if they can, we can. What do you think, Robert?"

Robert brushed back his hair from his forehead with a dirty hand. "All right. Have to admit you're a lot tougher than I thought you were."

Walter hoped Robert couldn't see how relieved he was that they were through fighting. He didn't know if he could have kept on.

"Thanks for jumping in and helping," Grant said when he and Walter were walking home.

"You did the same thing for me."

"They weren't hitting you at the time."

"They would have been if you hadn't stepped in when you did." Walter looked down at his torn shirt and knickers. "Boy, between this and the note about the book, my parents aren't going to be in a very good mood tonight."

Still, he couldn't help feeling good that he'd helped Grant.

He was glad Grant had helped him get out of a fight with Robert earlier in the week, but he'd been a bit embarrassed that he'd needed help. Now he and Grant were even.

He was sure glad to have such a good friend. And to think he'd been worried about meeting children when he moved here! The thought made him smile. "Ouch!"

Grant darted him a surprised look.

Walter touched his lip gingerly. It was split and bleeding. "Guess Robert left me something to remember our fight by."

CHAPTER 10
Learning the Territory

Robert left Walter with more than a split lip to remember the fight. He had a black eye, too.

Judith gaped at him when he entered the house. "What happened to you?"

"None of your business." Wouldn't you know his sister would see him right away? She'd be sure to tell their parents.

He could hear his mother working in the kitchen. He headed for the stairs and his bedroom, hoping to clean up before she saw him.

Judith was right on his heels. "You were in a fight, weren't you?"

"Go away."

"You were, I can tell. That's why your new school clothes are torn and your face looks like you are wounded."

"I'm not wounded. Go away." He walked into his room and slammed the door shut.

She opened it. "I'm going to tell Mama."

Walter whirled around. "Judith!"

Too late. He could hear his sister's footsteps racing down the hallway. With a groan, he flopped back onto his bed. Little sisters were so much trouble.

He stood up and looked in the mirror over the washstand. "Couldn't have hidden that I was in a fight, anyway," he muttered. His face was a mess, and his clothes were rumpled and torn.

He poured water from the pitcher into the china bowl and splashed water on his face, washing away the dirt and dried blood. When he was done, he looked in the mirror again and shook his head. "Doesn't look much better."

"Walter, come down here!" he heard his mother call from the bottom of the stairs.

He groaned again and headed for the stairs. It was easier to fight Robert than to face his mother. At least his father wasn't home yet.

Mama stood at the bottom of the stairs, wiping her hands on the work apron that covered her dress from shoulders to ankles. He walked down the stairs slowly.

His mother was usually patient, but she didn't like it when he tore clothes on tree limbs or got grass stains on the elbows of his shirts when he dove for a base playing baseball. She was sure to be upset over the torn school clothes.

He stood on the bottom step and bit his lip while she looked him over from head to toe. Then she closed her green eyes and shook her head. "Walter, what happened?"

Before he could answer, the back door slammed.

"Anybody home?" His father's cheerful voice boomed out.

Walter wished this were all a bad dream. The day kept getting worse!

The swinging door between the kitchen and dining room swung open. His father came out, still dressed in his work clothes and smelling like soot from the train. His brown eyes were sparkling with a smile. "Isn't anyone going to say hello to their papa?"

"Hello, Papa," Walter mumbled. His lip was swelling, and it was beginning to make his words sound funny.

Judith raced across the room and threw her arms around her father's waist. "Hello. Walter was in a fight."

"Judith, that is quite enough of that," their mother protested.

Walter thought so, too!

His father's smile turned into a frown as he looked Walter over. "It looks like Judith is right. What happened, Son?"

"There's this bully at school, Robert. He and his friend ganged up on Grant after school today. Two against one, you know?" Walter searched his father's face for a hint of sympathy.

His father nodded. "Two against one," he repeated.

"So–so I *had* to help Grant."

His father sighed deeply. "I suppose so." He leaned close and studied Walter's face, then winced. "You're sure going to feel those bruises tomorrow."

"We'll chip some ice from the block in the ice box to put on the bruises," his mother said. She shook her head again. "Your face will heal, but I'm not sure there's anything I can do to repair those clothes. We'll have to buy you new ones."

"You'll have to do extra chores to pay for them," his father said sternly.

"Yes, sir," Walter mumbled, lisping through his swelling lips. Now he'd have to pay for the book and new clothes, too, all because of Robert. "That reminds me, I almost forgot to give you the note from Miss Lee."

He dug the wrinkled piece of paper out of his pocket and handed it to his father. "I'll go get that ice."

He was almost to the kitchen door when he heard his father roar, "Walter, come back here!"

Things could have gone worse, Walter thought, sitting at his school desk two weeks later. He ran a finger beneath the starched white collar at the neck of the new suit of school clothes that replaced the ones he'd ruined in the fight with Robert.

His father had been angry about the book. "Do you really think we're going to believe all the trouble you get into is Robert's fault?"

Even so, his parents had said that since it wasn't like Walter to ruin schoolbooks, they would trust him this time. He still had to do extra chores to make up for the money his father had to pay for the book. *That's better than being told I couldn't do some of the things I like, like spending time with Grant.*

Walter glanced at Robert. At least since the fight, he didn't have to worry about staying out of Robert's way anymore. Robert had had some bruises from the fight, too, but both of their bruises were gone now.

Miss Lee rapped her pointing stick on her desk to get the class's attention. Walter obediently faced the front and waited for her to speak. He'd tried to do his best in class since she'd found the ink blot in his book.

"It's time for our geography lesson," Miss Lee said.

"Walter, why don't you draw us a map of Minnesota and Dakota and Montana Territories?"

Walter walked up to the large black slate on the wall at the front of the room. It seemed like she was always calling on him. Polly said it was because he was new at the school, and Miss Lee wanted to find out how much he knew.

Whatever the reason, I wish she would call on other students more and me less, he thought, starting to draw the outline of Minnesota.

"Make the drawing large, so the entire class can see it," Miss Lee ordered in her pleasant way.

When he was done, she asked the class, "Are Dakota and Montana states?"

Robert answered. "No. The Indians haven't sold most of that land to the United States."

"That's right. What do we call land the Indians haven't sold or given to the government or someone else?"

"Unceded," Grant answered. "Indians use the land, but other people sometimes use it, too."

"Correct. Is that the same as a reservation?"

Grant shook his head. "No. Reservations are lands that belong only to Indians. The United States government has agreed that other people won't use that land."

"That's right, Grant. The government promises they will give Indians who live on the reservation food, since there isn't always enough game on the reservations for the Indians to feed their people." She turned back to the wall slate, where Walter still stood. "Mark the Black Hills on the map, Walter."

Walter made some squiggly lines along the western portion of the lower part of Dakota.

"Who knows why white people want to go to the Black Hills?" Miss Lee asked.

Almost everyone in class raised their hands. "The gold rush!" several students called out.

"Why does that make the Indians angry?" she asked.

"Because the Black Hills are on an Indian reservation," Robert's friend answered.

"And the Black Hills are sacred ground to the Indians," Grant added.

Miss Lee nodded. "Chiefs from Sioux, Cheyenne, and Arapahe nations have just signed an agreement with the United States."

That was the agreement that Bishop Whipple had worked on, Walter remembered.

"It says," she continued, "that the Sioux will receive no more food from the United States government unless they give certain unceded land and the Black Hills to the United States, let the government build three roads across their reservations to the Black Hills, and agree to become farmers." She pointed to the Black Hills on Walter's map. "The land the Indians are asked to give up includes the Black Hills and all the land west of it."

Walter looked at his map. "That's a lot of land. Do the settlers need all that land?"

Miss Lee smiled. "Maybe not right away, but the government wants to be sure it will be safe for people to settle in that part of the country if they choose to do so."

A girl in the first row raised her hand. "What does the government promise to give the Indians if the Indians give them their land and become farmers?"

"That's a very good question, Amy. The government will help them build houses and schools on the reservation. It will also give them food for their families while they are learning how to farm. And other people will not be allowed on their reservations without their permission."

"The treaty the government already had with the Sioux said other people aren't allowed on their reservation," Grant said, "but the government lets miners into the Black Hills anyway." His voice was loud and angry.

Walter looked at him in surprise. Grant was usually quiet and well behaved in class.

"Yes, Grant," Miss Lee said in a quiet voice, "but the United States government has to protect its own people. Whenever a country has to choose between protecting their people or the people of another nation, the government must protect its own people first."

Grant snorted, crossed his arms, and leaned back.

"Besides," she continued, "the new agreement has been made to punish the Indians, remember? When people are punished, they often have to give up something."

Like doing extra chores to pay for my new school clothes and the book Robert ruined, Walter thought.

Grant glared at Miss Lee. "Under the old treaty, the government agreed the Indians could hunt on unceded land. For as far back as the oldest Indian can remember, their people have spent the summers following game and hunting so they would have food. When Custer attacked the Indians, the Indians were only doing what they were allowed to do under the treaty."

Walter shifted about uncomfortably. Except for Grant, the class was as still as a house after everyone has gone to bed.

Miss Lee sighed. "Last summer the government told the Indians they were to stay on their reservations rather than hunt on the unceded land, remember? That's why the cavalry attacked the Indians—because they didn't stay on the reservation."

Grant leaped to his feet. "Why can the government take back a promise it made under a treaty? It's not right to break promises," he yelled. "It's not fair!"

Walter heard a number of students gasp. His own jaw dropped, and his stomach clenched. Students were never allowed to yell at a teacher!

Miss Lee's eyes snapped with anger, but she didn't raise her voice. "That is quite enough, Grant. You will sit down."

"But the Indians aren't being treated fairly!"

Robert looked at Grant and sneered. "Indian lover!"

"Indian lover! Indian lover!" A number of students picked up Robert's taunt.

Miss Lee rapped her stick against the desk so hard Walter thought it would break. "Stop it, all of you!"

Some of the students stopped, but not all.

"I said stop it!" Miss Lee yelled to make herself heard.

Walter stared at her. He'd never heard a teacher yell before! Her face was as red as a beet.

The rest of the class must have been as shocked as Walter to hear gentle Miss Lee holler, because everyone immediately stopped talking and stared at her.

"That's better." She yanked at the wrists of her blouse. "Since you all seem to have such strong opinions on the Indian issue, you may all tell me about them. You are each to write a three-page essay on 'Treaties Between the United States and the Indian Nations.' It will be due Monday."

"Monday!" Robert protested. "But today's Friday."

"Monday." She glared at Robert. "And since you and Grant are the most opinionated of all the students, you may write from each others' point of view. You, Robert, will write showing the Indians' side of the issue. You, Grant, will show the government's."

"But, Miss Lee," Robert argued, "I wasn't the one who yelled. It was that Indian lover Grant. I shouldn't have to—"

"In addition," she interrupted him, "Grant and Robert shall stay after school to begin their essays."

"But, Miss Lee—" Robert started.

She fixed him with an icy glare. "I can make the punishment worse if you like, Robert."

Robert crossed his arms over his chest and slumped in his chair.

Miss Lee took a deep breath. "Now, we shall go on to our arithmetic lesson. I'll hear no more about the Indian issue today."

Walter took his seat as Miss Lee called on Amy, the girl in the first row, to recite her multiplication sums, beginning with fives.

Amy began the singsong chant. "Five times one is five. Five times two is ten."

Walter's thoughts weren't on multiplication. He glanced at Robert's angry face, and an uneasy feeling wound through his chest. He didn't think Robert was going to be friendly with him and Grant anymore.

When school was over, Walter stopped by Grant's desk. "I'd wait for you, but I have to get home and do chores."

"That's all right."

"I think you were brave to say those things about the Indians today. Why don't you come over to my house tonight and we can work on our essays together?" He grinned. "Even if you will have a head start on me."

Grant gave him a small smile.

When Walter met Grant at the door that evening, his stomach did a somersault. A huge purple bruise covered Grant's cheek.

CHAPTER 11

Letters to the President

Walter gasped. "What happened to you?"

Grant gently touched the bruise on his cheek. "Robert and his two creepy friends happened. They caught me alone after school." He gave a harsh laugh. "Turns out they don't like 'Indian lovers.' Isn't that a surprise?"

"Chicken hearts. They only start fights when it's two or more against one."

Together they walked into the family sitting room. Walter had already lit the kerosene lamp on the table in the middle of the room where he and Grant would work on their essays.

Mama was seated in her favorite chair, a rocker. Judith was seated on a small footstool beside her. She bit the bottom of her lip as she concentrated on the sock Mama was teaching her to darn.

Papa sat in the most comfortable chair in the room and was reading the newspaper. He looked up when the boys walked in. "Looks like you've been in a scuffle, Grant."

"Guess who it was with?" Walter said. "Robert."

Grant and Walter told Papa and Mama the story behind the fight and the essays.

"Sounds to me like Robert has a lot to learn," Papa said. "A man can't make other people think like him by fighting."

Mama shook her head and went back to her darning. "I wish he'd learn his lesson soon and leave these boys alone."

Grant set his writing tablet on the table, and both boys sat down and began working. After a few minutes, Walter said, "I thought with Bishop Whipple helping with the Indian agreement, the Indians would be treated more fairly."

The paper rustled as Papa set it down. "When there are battles and wars between nations, the treaties never seem fair to the people who lose. The strongest nation gets the most under a treaty."

"But if Bishop Whipple likes the Indians and he wants good things for them, why didn't he make the agreement better for them?" Walter asked.

Papa spread his big hands. "One man can't do everything by himself. There was a whole group of men who wrote the agreement the government offered the Indians. For all we know, if Bishop Whipple and good men like him weren't helping with the agreement, it could have been worse."

Grant hooked an arm over the back of his chair and turned to look at Papa. "They should have let the Indians keep using unceded land and keep their old ways of getting food and other things for their families if they wanted to. Why should

96

they have to live on just a little land, like other people, and be farmers? It isn't fair."

"No, it probably isn't fair," Papa agreed. "I think the reason Bishop Whipple and the other men made the agreement the way they did is because they believe if the Indians don't choose to live like other people, the other people will kill all the Indians."

"I wish there was something I could do to change people's minds," Walter said.

"When you want the government to change the way they are doing something, you have to tell the people in the government," Papa said.

"Like the president?" Walter asked.

"Yes."

Walter turned to Grant. "Let's write to President Grant!"

"Why should he listen to a couple of children?"

"President Lincoln listened to Bishop Whipple after the Sioux Uprising, didn't he?" Walter asked. "It can't hurt to write to him."

Papa slapped his hands on his knees. "I think that's a great idea."

"You can write your letters this weekend," Mama said, "after you finish your homework."

"Maybe we can talk Polly and Brita into writing to the president, too." Walter was excited about the idea now.

"Did you two remember to read the newspaper tonight?" Papa asked, holding it out to them. "There's an article in it that I think Polly will want to see."

Walter and Grant spread the newspaper on the table and glanced through the headlines. It didn't take long for them to spot the one that Walter's father was talking about.

" 'Jessie James's Cronies Captured,' " Walter read. He

and Grant bent their heads over the article.

The next morning when Walter stopped at Polly's house, Polly was sitting at the sewing machine in the family sitting room. Mounds of yellow material spilled over the top of the machine and onto the floor. Polly's high-buttoned shoe pressed in a fast, even motion on the machine's fancy brass peddle, making the needle move up and down through the material with a speed no woman could match by hand.

She looked up from the sewing machine with a bright smile. "Did you hear?" she asked before he could tell her the news. "Some of the bank robbers were captured."

Walter laughed. "That's what I came to tell you." It was good to see her happy again.

A small frown creased her brow. "Jesse James and his brother, Frank, got away. The robbers that were captured said the James brothers stole horses and rode out of Minnesota."

"Yes, so your father and his bank won't be in any danger from them."

"I hope not. Sometimes I think living somewhere like Cincinnati would be nice. Maybe it would be safer than living here."

"Minneapolis isn't so bad," Walter admitted, surprised to find he really felt that way. "Besides," he added with a grin, "the James brothers found out that law-abiding people in Minnesota are too tough for them. They won't be back."

Polly laughed with him. She lifted a fold of the yellow material. "I'm making a new school dress. Mother is helping me with the hardest parts. She bought yards and yards of lace and ribbon for it. It's going to be very fashionable!"

"That's nice." Walter couldn't see why girls got so excited about clothes, especially when they had to work so hard to make them, but if it made her happy, that was all right with him.

"Grant and I are going to write letters to President Grant tonight about the Indian wars and treaties. We don't like what's happening to the Indians. Do you want to come over and write one, too?"

Polly frowned. "I'm not so sure," she said slowly. "I don't think the Indians are treated fairly, but I can see why people are afraid of them. Look what happened to Brita and Per's family."

"That was a long time ago, before we were born. Besides, you don't have to write all the same things Grant and I write. You can tell the president what *you* think."

"All right. Maybe we should ask Lars if he will write a letter, too."

Walter thought that was a good idea. "I don't think I'll ask Brita and Per, though. They wouldn't stand up for the Indians' side!"

Walter was disappointed when Lars said he wouldn't write a letter to the president, either.

"Why not?" Walter asked. "Don't you think the Indians should be treated better?"

"Yah, but I don't write English good." Lars looked up from the boots he was polishing. "I would be embarrassed for a great man like the president to see how bad I write and spell."

"Your English has gotten a lot better since I met you," Walter encouraged.

"Not so very good. I am not getting good grades. It is hard when everything is in English."

"Wasn't it hard where you went to school out by your farm, too?" Walter asked.

"When we moved to the farm, we met at a neighbor's sod house for school. All the children were Swedish, so we learned in Swedish. Then Father said we must learn in English. 'You live in America now. You must speak as they speak, or life will be hard,' he told us. But the school we went to wasn't big like the one here, and we didn't have all the good schoolbooks."

As always, Walter had to listen carefully to understand Lars, even though he spoke slowly, trying to get the words right.

"What was it like where you went to school?" Walter asked.

"When we couldn't meet at the sod house anymore, we boys that wanted more schooling looked for a place to hold class. We found a shanty a farmer had abandoned that was almost falling down. We asked the school board if they would hire a teacher for us if we fixed it up, and they did."

"You had to repair your own school?" Walter couldn't believe it.

Lars nodded. "There were holes in the walls and floor that were so big that polecats could crawl inside. We had to cover the holes so snow and wind couldn't blow into the shanty. We made our own desks and a desk for the teacher. There wasn't a slate like we have on the walls at the school here, so we boys pounded some boards together and painted them black."

"Did you have schoolbooks?"

"Only a few. We had to share them. We were lucky to have a dictionary. Not all the schools in our county had dictionaries. We didn't have any maps or globes for geography, either."

Walter couldn't imagine what it must have been like trying to learn with hardly any books.

100

"We couldn't go to school much, anyway. On homesteads like ours, boys have to work hard to help their fathers farm the land and take care of the animals. Mostly we boys went to school for two or three months in the winter, when there wasn't as much work to do on the farm."

No wonder he doesn't speak and write English well, Walter thought.

Lars sighed. "I've been studying the English-Swedish dictionary at home every night. If my English gets better, I can learn faster."

An idea popped into Walter's head. "Maybe I can help you with your English."

A grin lit up Lars's face. "Would you?"

"Sure."

Lars jumped up, the boot he'd been polishing dropping to the floor with a thud. "I'll get my dictionary."

Walter started to say something, then stopped. Lars was already in the other room. "I didn't mean right now," Walter mumbled to himself, "but I guess that's all right."

Lars was back in a minute, his blue eyes snapping with excitement beneath his almost-white blond hair. "I'm having trouble with the *k* words."

Walter frowned. "Why?"

"I don't know when to say the *k* sound and when the *k* is silent." He picked up a knife from the cupboard. "Like this. When I told another student at school that I needed a knife, he laughed at me."

Walter couldn't help laughing, either. Lars had pronounced the word *k-nife.*

Lars smiled. "It's funny to me, too, now that I *k-now* how to say knife the right way."

Walter laughed harder.

Lars frowned. "You don't have to laugh so much."

"Sorry, but it sounds so funny to hear you say *k-nife* and *k-now.*"

Lars got a funny look on his face. "Oh. Is *k-now* another of the *k* words?"

Walter nodded, still unable to stop grinning.

"See what I mean?" Lars sighed. "I'll never learn the *k* words."

"I never realized how hard it must be to learn English," Walter admitted. "I don't think there's a rule you can learn to tell you which words have silent *k*s. Why don't you just ask me when you see a new *k* word?"

"Yah, I'll just do that."

"Um, there's something I've been wondering ever since I moved to Minneapolis. Why do the Swedish people say *j*s like *y*s? Can't Swedish people say the *j* sound?" Walter asked.

His face grew red from embarrassment when Lars laughed.

"Sure we can say the *j* sound. But in the Swedish language, the *j* is pronounced like the *y* in English. We forget to say it like your *j*, that's all."

"Oh." Now it was Walter's turn to feel foolish. "I guess we're both going to learn things if I help you with English." He grinned. "I'll keep reminding you about the *j* sound."

He stood up, ready to leave for home and his chores. "Say, maybe you'll teach me some Swedish words while I help you with your English. It would be fun to know another language."

"Yah, sure."

CHAPTER 12

Search for Gold

As Walter, Grant, and Lars reached the school grounds one morning late in October, Robert and his friends met them. They stood on the high flight of stairs at the front of the school and stared down at Walter and his friends.

"Hey, Indian lover, did you hear the good news about the Sioux chief Sitting Bull and his warriors?" Robert perched his hands on his hips and grinned.

Walter glared at Robert. *Why does he always have to try picking fights?* he wondered, but he just kept climbing the stairs. So did Grant and Lars.

Robert and his friends spread out across the steps. They

put their hands on their hips so their arms filled the space between them.

Walter and his friends stopped and waited for the others to move.

They didn't move.

"I asked you a question, Indian lover," Robert said. "Did you hear about the cavalry attacking Chief Sitting Bull and his warriors?"

"I heard." Grant stuck out his chin and stared back at Robert. In one hand Grant held his book strap, which was buckled around his schoolbooks. Walter saw his other hand tighten into a fist at his side.

"Two thousand of the warriors surrendered to the cavalry." Robert grinned again. "What do you think of that?"

Grant stuck his fist in his trouser pocket. "Did you hear that Chief Sitting Bull and some of his warriors escaped?"

"The cavalry will find them," Robert said. His two friends snickered. "The cavalry told Sioux chief Red Cloud he's not a chief anymore, too."

Grant's face grew red. Walter wondered uneasily how much more Robert would have to say before Grant took a swing at him.

"The cavalry didn't make Red Cloud a chief, and it can't take away his position as a chief," Grant said.

"The cavalry took away his guns and horse and his warriors' guns and horses. He can't be a very powerful chief." Robert laughed, and the sound of it made Walter want to punch him in the face.

"Fighting isn't the only thing that makes a chief powerful," Walter told him. "President Grant doesn't fight, and he's got a lot of power. Red Cloud's words make him powerful. He speaks for the Sioux to our country's leaders."

"Red Cloud speaks for peace between the Indians and white people," Grant reminded them. "He wants the Indians to live freely on their lands but tells them the United States has too many people for the Indians to fight."

"He isn't going to get peace." Robert stepped down so he was only one step above Grant. "Like General Sherman said, 'The only good Indian is a dead Indian.' "

Grant grabbed Robert's arm and pulled.

"Hey! Let go!" Robert lost his balance and fell down the steps.

A bunch of children who had been watching the argument started laughing. Robert jumped to his feet, his face red with anger.

Walter's stomach tightened. *Oh, no,* he thought, *not another fight.* Robert would never stand for being embarrassed in front of the other students.

Robert pushed back the sleeves of his wool jacket and started up the stairs, his eyes flashing.

Out of the corner of his eye, Walter saw Robert's friends move close together to block Grant from going up the steps and into the school.

Fear slithered through Walter's chest. He didn't want to fight again, but it looked like there wasn't going to be a choice. Keeping his gaze on Robert's friends, he let go of his book strap. The books thudded onto the steps.

He saw Grant start to swing his books by his book strap. Back and forth. Robert hesitated. Grant's books would make quite a weapon if Robert attacked him, Walter realized.

On the other side of Grant, Lars was standing his ground, but Walter could see fear in his face.

One of Robert's friends pushed Grant, and he fell right into Robert, knocking both of them to the ground at the bottom of the stairs. Suddenly fists were flying, and Walter couldn't tell whose fists were landing the most.

He dodged one of Robert's friends' fists and rushed down the stairs. He was reaching for Robert's jacket when a large hand pushed him aside and another jerked Robert right up off the ground.

Walter looked up in surprise. The school superintendent!

The man kept hold of the neck of Robert's jacket and reached down to yank Grant up by his arm. He held the boys so high that they had to stand on tiptoe.

"I'll have no fighting on school grounds," he growled through his neatly cut beard. "Go clean the dirt off your faces and get to class. If I catch you at this again, you'll be suspended."

He let go of both boys at once and stalked up the stairs.

Grant brushed the dirt from his jacket.

Robert brushed dirt from his trousers. "I'll get you later, when there's not any old superintendent around."

Walter and Grant walked up the steps together, picking up their books on the way. Lars was still standing there and walked into school with them.

Walter glanced back at Robert and his friends and the crowd of children beyond them in the schoolyard. Suddenly a warm feeling filled his chest. He remembered when he started school and he'd wanted to make lots of new friends. He knew lots of students now, and most of them were friendly toward him, but he wouldn't call them good friends. A guy didn't need lots of best friends. Not when he had a couple friends like Grant and Lars.

Robert slid in behind his side of the desk as the bell for class rang. He leaned over and whispered, "You an Indian lover, too, Fisk?"

"I like fair play."

"You'd better watch your back."

A shiver slithered up Walter's spine, but he just stared back at Robert. "You guys couldn't beat me and Grant together last time. You never will be able to beat us one-on-one."

"Don't be too sure."

Miss Lee called the class to attention, and Walter turned away from Robert.

The hate he'd heard in Robert's voice made his heart race. *But I won't run away from him ever again,* Walter thought. *From now on I'm going to stick up for what I believe in, like Grant, no matter what happens.*

That evening Walter went over to Brita and Per's house to help Lars with his English. As he and Lars sat together at a table in the family room, he glanced about at the others. It was always fun to go to their home. With so many children in the house, it was a friendly, warm-hearted place to be.

As in most of the homes Walter knew, the parlor was used only for special company. Everyone gathered in the family living room in the evenings. Even though the house had a coal-burning furnace like Walter's house, there was a fireplace in the family room. The popping and cracking of the wood as yellow and blue flames danced made the room cheerful.

Brita was knitting a muffler, getting ready for winter.

Mrs. Swenson and Lars's mother rocked back and forth in oak rockers while they chatted and darned socks. Sometimes they talked in Swedish and sometimes in English. Sometimes they mixed both languages in their sentences.

Mr. Swenson was in an overstuffed chair, reading a news-paper written in Swedish. Walter knew his own father was doing the same thing at his house, only his newspaper was in English.

He laughed at Lars's brother and sister, four-year-old Axel and six-year-old Kirstin, who were busy rummaging through Mrs. Larson's colorful tin button box. The box was filled to the brim with spare buttons of every size, shape, and color. The children were taking their favorites and threading them together into necklaces.

"I used to do that when I was little," Walter told Lars.

Lars looked up from his English-Swedish dictionary and glanced at his brother and sister. "Yah, me too."

"When I moved to Minneapolis, I thought Swedish families were different from us. Some things you do are different, but mostly our families are a lot alike."

Lars grinned.

Per came in with an armful of logs and dropped them in the wooden box beside the fireplace. A minute later, he pulled out a wooden chair and sat down with Lars and Walter. "I hear you two and Polly have been writing to the president, Walter."

Walter nodded, smiling.

"Don't you know that it will help the railroads your father works for if the Indians move onto reservations?"

Walter frowned. "How?"

"If the Indians aren't using the unceded land anymore, then the railroads can lay tracks across that land. The railroad companies will make a lot of money carrying settlers like Lars's family to the new land and carrying their crops and livestock to market."

"I never thought of that," Walter said slowly.

Per folded his arms on the tabletop. "Soldiers won't have to guard the men while they lay tracks for the new railroad lines, either, like they have to now."

Were the railroads one of the reasons the government was trying to shove all the Indians onto reservations? Walter wondered.

A strange feeling curled in his stomach. He knew his father didn't like the way the Indians were being treated. Still, Walter had never felt guilty before because his father worked for the railroad. He didn't like the feeling at all.

CHAPTER 13

A Day of Prayer

April sunshine shone brightly down on Grant's backyard as Grant, Walter, and Lars practiced their pitching.

Walter finally dropped to the ground in disgust. "We've been practicing since last Fourth of July, and we still can't throw curveballs."

"At least you saw the pitcher throw curveballs," Lars said. "I've never seen it done."

"It was great." Walter stared at the sky, remembering.

"Maybe you can go to a baseball match with us this summer, Lars," Grant encouraged.

"I don't think so. My family will be moving back to the homestead in a few weeks to be with *Far* and brother."

"Already?" Grant asked. "Before school is out?"

Lars nodded. *"Mor* says we should be there now, helping Father get the land plowed and planted."

Walter and Grant exchanged looks. Things wouldn't be the same without Lars around. They'd become good friends during the winter months.

"Maybe you can visit us sometime," Walter suggested. "It would be fun to all go to a baseball match and watch Minneapolis's new team, the Brown Stockings."

"The new pitcher is the one from Massachusetts who threw the curveballs last year," Grant reminded them.

Walter sighed and wrapped his arms around his knees. "It will be fun to watch him play—and he'll probably win a lot of matches for Minneapolis—but I'll miss Captain Smith."

"I will, too, but he's not as good a pitcher as the new man," Grant said practically.

Walter straightened his spine and snapped his fingers. "Hey, I just thought of something! If the grasshoppers are bad again this year, maybe your dad will send you and your family back to Minneapolis, Lars. Then you can go to a game with us." He spread his hands, palms upward. "Something good can come of anything bad."

Lars smiled, but shook his head. The spring sunshine glinted off his blond hair. "As much as I'd like to see a curveball thrown, I don't want to see any grasshoppers this year. I've seen enough to last a lifetime. I hope God answers people's prayers tomorrow."

Governor Pillsbury had declared a day of fasting and prayer. He said people in Minnesota were to ask God to forgive the sins of Minnesota and the United States and ask Him to keep the grasshoppers away from farmers' crops this year.

"Does Brita and Per's father have tomorrow off work?" Walter asked Lars.

"No. Only the flour mills Governor Pillsbury owns are closed tomorrow so the men can go to church. Everyone still has to work at the flour mill where my uncle works, so we're going to church after supper."

"I'm thirsty." Grant picked up the baseball they'd been playing with and headed for the back door of his house. "Let's get a drink of water."

The water rushing from the pump at the iron kitchen sink was cold and clear and felt wonderful going down Walter's parched throat. He and the others sat down beside the kitchen table to talk for a few minutes while they finished their water.

One thing Walter had noticed about Grant's house: there were never any baked goods like cookies around for snacks like there were at most of the homes he knew. He supposed that was because Grant and his father lived alone and didn't have any women to cook for them.

While they talked, Walter played idly with a thick, small, leather-covered book that lay on the table. It was just something to do with his fingers. He didn't pay any attention to the book at first.

Then he realized—the book was a Bible. Not just any Bible. It was written in another language. *What language*? he wondered. Grant's father was French. Maybe the Bible was written in French.

"Is this a French Bible, Grant?"

"No. It's written in the Sioux language."

Walter's jaw dropped. So did Lars's.

Walter turned a few pages and tried to read a few words. Lars peered over his shoulder.

"I suppose one of your father or grandfather's Sioux friends gave this to him, huh?" Walter asked.

Grant didn't answer. Instead he asked a question. "Did you know who first asked Governor Pillsbury to declare a day of prayer to get rid of the grasshoppers?"

"Who?" Lars asked.

"The Christian Sioux."

Walter looked up from the book, surprised and pleased. "That was a good idea."

"I think it's a good idea that we get out of school for it," Lars said.

Walter and Grant agreed.

There were special church services in the morning, afternoon, and evening the next day, so everyone had a time they could go, even if they had to work.

Walter glanced about the sanctuary while he waited with his family for the service to begin. All kinds of people were there: the mayor, the governor, teachers, Polly's family, and neighbors who worked at the railroad, flour mills, and lumber mills. Grant had come with Walter's family, since his father had to work.

Even Robert was there with his family, Walter saw with surprise. He didn't think Robert acted like a boy who loved Jesus.

Lars, Brita, and Per's families weren't there. They attended a church where other Swedish families went, but Walter knew they were in church for prayer, too.

Walter wasn't surprised when the pastor said the people had to ask God to forgive them and their state and their country for all their sins. He already knew that. But he was surprised to hear what the pastor thought people were doing wrong.

"Is it any wonder God has allowed the crops in our state and country to be attacked by grasshoppers?" the bearded pastor asked, leaning on the wooden pulpit at the front of the church. "We have treated the Indian nations, the people to whom God first gave these lands, as though they do not belong in America."

Walter and Grant looked at each other in surprise, then leaned forward to listen more closely.

The pastor told the congregation some of the same things that Grant had told their class at school: that the Indians had kept the promises they'd made in their treaties, but the white people hadn't kept their promises.

"Now maybe somebody will listen," Grant whispered. "No one listens to a boy, it seems."

At the end of his sermon, the pastor said, "Many people say we must kill all Indians to make our country safe. God will not allow all the Indians to be killed. God has a purpose for the Indians, the same as He has a purpose for each of us in this church, and for our state, and for our country."

"What do you think God's purpose for the Indian nations is?" Walter asked Grant when they were back outside.

"I don't know."

I wonder what it is, Walter thought.

Polly caught up to them, wearing the pretty yellow dress she'd made the previous fall. White lace, ribbons, and bows covered the front of the dress and wrists of the sleeves.

"Do you think God will answer everyone's prayers and keep the grasshoppers away?" she asked.

"I hope so," Walter said. "Farmers need their crops. The grasshoppers have made them very poor."

"Brita and I and our mothers are working on another quilt to send to the grasshopper counties," Polly said. "It's fun to work on quilts, but I wish people didn't need them so badly."

"Do you think God sent the grasshoppers to punish settlers for the way the Indians have been treated?" Grant asked.

"Maybe." Walter watched one of spring's first robins watching them from a tree branch. "But why would He punish settlers like Lars's family, who didn't have anything to do with moving the Indians out of Minnesota or with sending the cavalry to attack the Indians?"

"Maybe the Indians are just one reason God let the grasshoppers make so much trouble," Polly suggested.

"I wonder if God will answer everyone's prayers," Grant said quietly.

Walter wondered, too. It would be wonderful to see God work a miracle and keep the grasshoppers away.

The next evening, the warm sunny spring days had turned cold again. It both rained and snowed.

Was this God's way of answering the people's prayers? Would the cold kill the grasshopper eggs that the grasshoppers had laid in the fields last summer? No one would know for a while, but everyone hoped so.

But a month later Grant complained, "I hoped the sermons would make people change the way the Indians are being treated, but they didn't. Instead the cavalry killed Chief Lame Deer, and three thousand Indians who were living on unceded lands have surrendered and moved to reservations. Chief Crazy Horse even surrendered!"

The unfairness of it all left Walter feeling empty and hopeless. "At least people are beginning to understand that everything wasn't the Indians' fault. They are hearing the truth about the way the Indians have been treated."

"There are hardly any Sioux and Cheyenne that haven't surrendered and agreed to live on the reservations now. Before Custer attacked the Indians last summer, there were thousands living as they've always lived, living where they had to live to find food for their families."

"Father says things between the cavalry and Indians have gone too far. He says it's like a snowball. If you start a small snowball at the top of a hill, it picks up snow as it rolls down and becomes bigger and harder to stop. No one seems to know how to stop what's happening."

"No one," Grant agreed with a sad face.

CHAPTER 14

The Fishing Trip

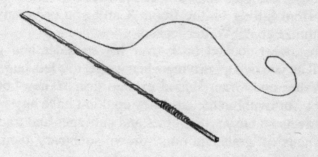

"Fishing? Sure we want to go!" Walter told his father.

"Right now?" Grant asked his own father.

Mr. LaPierre's grin shown through his thick dark beard. "Right now. I've brought the cane fishing poles."

"And a frying pan," Walter's father added. "We're going to catch and cook our own meal today."

"Whoopee!" Walter dropped the baseball he and Grant had been tossing back and forth and headed for the shed to get poles for himself and his father.

With school out for the summer, Walter and Grant spent as much time as possible on their riverside trails or practicing their baseball. Some days they'd sit on the warm rocks at the river's edge, fish, and pretend they were Tom Sawyer and his friend Huckleberry Finn. But that wasn't the same as going fishing with the men.

Walter and Grant, both grinning ear to ear, climbed up in the back seat of the buggy Papa had rented for the outing. "Too bad Lars isn't here to go with us," Grant said.

Walter thought so, too. He missed the quiet Swedish boy since Lars had gone back to the farm. Would Lars miss Minneapolis and his friends here?

The buggy lurched as a wheel hit a hole in the dirt street. The boys grabbed the back of the seat in front of them to keep from falling on the floor. "Can't you drive any better than that, Papa?" Walter teased.

His father looked back over his shoulder and grinned. "We'll let you two try driving when we get to a less busy street."

Walter and Grant shared excited grins. They both liked horses, but living in the city, they couldn't have any. With the city streets so busy with horses and carriages and traders and merchants' wagons and horse-drawn streetcars, their fathers didn't let them drive the buggies often.

The buggy ride was jerky. It had rained the last couple days, and the road had more ruts and holes than usual. They passed a street worker repairing the road as they always did after a storm. The worker's horse pulled a log behind it to smooth the ruts. A shovel was tied on the horse's back for the worker to use to fill in deep holes.

Walter watched eagerly for a sight of Lake Calhoun through the trees. He'd heard lots of people talk about Lake Calhoun. There were many smaller lakes he'd been to around Minneapolis, but he'd never seen this lake.

He and Grant ran up and down the dock while their fathers arranged to rent a boat. Swarms of minnows swam in the shadows and weeds beneath the dock. Water bugs spread their wide legs and drifted along. Farther out, gulls floated, watching for dinner.

Walter took a deep breath. He liked the fishy smell of the lake and watching the birds and seeing the sunshine glint off the water and make it look like it was covered in diamonds.

After a long discussion of the best places to fish, the men decided to try an area near a large patch of bulrushes a long ways from where they'd rented the boat. Walter didn't think it mattered. All the times they'd been fishing in Minnesota, they'd caught more fish than they could eat.

They all took turns rowing. Walter's arms ached by the time they reached the rushes, but he wouldn't have admitted it for the world.

A long nightcrawler curled around his hand when he pulled it out of the jar filled with moist black dirt to put it on his hook. The men were arguing again in a friendly manner about the best bait to use. The boys laughed at their fathers and dropped their lines in the water. "We came to fish, not argue," Walter told them.

After half an hour, they already had a dozen good-sized fish, but they didn't quit. Walter knew they'd take any fish they didn't eat back home to share with the rest of their families and neighbors.

The sun beat down and warmed them, but they all had wide-brimmed hats to keep their faces shaded.

Walter liked the way the men talked easily with them about baseball and the new suspension bridge across the Mississippi River and how President Rutherford Hayes was doing in his first year as president and how important it was for men of every nation to fight for what they believe is important. At home, he and his father never seemed to have time to talk like that.

Mr. LaPierre told them what it was like growing up as a trapper's son. How cold it was in winter when he had to follow the trapline along a northern river and use a dogsled and snowshoes to get around the snow-covered countryside. How awful the mosquitoes were in the summer. How they tanned the skins and sewed fur hats, and how the Indians had taught him and his father how to make winter moccasins, with the animal skins on the outside and the fur on the inside.

"That's number twenty-four," Walter said as he pulled in another large fish.

His father, who had been leaning against the bow of the boat, pushed himself to a sitting position. "Hate to say it, but I think we'd better quit for the day. Even after we fry our fill of fish, we're going to have a hard time lugging the rest home."

Mr. LaPierre grinned through his beard. "The man may not rent any more buggies to you after he gets a whiff of the smell the fish will leave in the buggy today."

Walter and Grant laughed.

Mr. LaPierre pointed out a spot he said would be perfect for their cookout. Walter and Grant volunteered to row them to shore.

They jumped out of the boat when it ran aground and pulled it up on the grassy bank.

"Help us gather some stones and branches for a fire, boys," Mr. LaPierre said.

Grant taught Walter how to line the fireplace area with stones to prevent the fire from spreading to nearby grass and vines. "My father taught me this," he said. When they were done, Papa started a fire.

"We should have time to explore the shore while our fathers clean the fish," Grant told Walter. "The fire has to burn down to coals before they can cook the fish, anyway."

"Sounds like fun."

As soon as their fathers gave permission, Grant swung an arm toward a wooded area a little way down the shoreline. "Come on. There's a great place down this way I want to show you."

Walter followed him along the bank. Soon Grant pointed out a faint path along the bank and other paths that met it coming across meadows or through the woods. "These are trails of animals who come here to drink. See the deer tracks in the mud? And the raccoon tracks?"

Walter studied the trails. Some were so faint that he couldn't figure out how Grant had even been able to recognize them.

Some places the bank was covered with grass. At other places, trees grew right at the bank's edge and their branches hung out over the water. Walter recognized plum trees at one place. At another, the boys stopped and picked gooseberries. They had to fight mosquitoes and thorns to pick them.

Walter bit down on one of the hard green berries. A burst of sour juice squirted into his mouth. "Augh!" He scrunched up his face.

Grant laughed. "Don't you like them?"

"They're pretty sour." But Walter ate another one just the same. He liked eating food he found growing wild.

"Remember the missionaries I told you about who copied the Bible into the Sioux language?" Grant asked, ducking under a low tree branch.

"Like the Bible you showed us at your house? Yes."

"Samuel and Gideon Pond did that. Before they did that— almost forty years ago—they had a mission on this lake where they told the Sioux in Chief Cloudman's village about Jesus."

Walter stood on the bank and looked out across the lake,

121

trying to imagine a village filled with tipis and Indian families. Where were the children and grandchildren of the people who had lived in that village?

They rounded a bend to a small bay sheltered from the winds that blew across the lake. The water in the bay was calm. There was a sandy shore with wild grass growing along it here and there. Clam shells lay at the water's edge.

Walter liked the quiet. He liked the sound of the waves lapping against the shore, birds calling to each other, squirrels chattering, and insects singing. A red-winged blackbird sat on a bulrush, bending it over. A crane stood in the water, lifting its long legs carefully as it searched for fish.

The trunk of a huge tree that had fallen into the water tempted Walter, and he climbed out along it. He could see all the way to the bottom of the lake.

Near the tree were some large gray rocks. The water splashed gently against them. Two turtles, one large and one small, were sunning themselves on the rocks.

Grant followed him out on the tree. "Let's go swimming," he said.

At the sound of his voice, the turtles slipped off the rocks and underneath the water.

"Go swimming here? We'll get our clothes wet."

"We can take most of them off."

Walter hesitated. "It *is* hot out. The water would feel awfully good."

Two minutes later, all the boys' clothes except their drawers were piled on shore. They raced into the water, shrieking at the sudden cold. They had splashing fights, raced each other to the rocks the turtles had sunned themselves on, and dove after small rocks they saw on the bottom of the lake.

When they were tired out, they tried to pull themselves up on the rocks. They couldn't. Moss covered part of the rocks, making them slippery. So they climbed up on the tree instead. The rough bark and many branches made the tree easy to climb.

"Let's dive off," Grant said after they'd rested.

"That's dangerous. We might hit a rock or a log or something."

"We could jump off instead, where we can see the bottom." Grant stood up, being careful to hold on to a small branch.

Snap! The branch broke.

"Aaaaugh!"

Grant tottered a moment, his arms flailing, his eyes large in surprise.

Walter grabbed for him. Too late! His fingertips brushed the wet drawers on one of Grant's legs as Grant tumbled backward.

Splash! Grant hit the water. The splash from his fall showered water over Walter.

Walter burst into laughter. Grant looked so funny! Like a circus performer doing tumbling tricks.

"Good one, Grant! Your eyes and mouth were so big, you looked like one of the fish we caught!" He turned around on the wide trunk to see Grant.

Grant was underneath the water. Still grinning, Walter waited a minute for him to come up.

It only took a moment for Walter to see that Grant wasn't coming up. His body was floating under the water near a large submerged rock. Something dark was starting to cloud the water near Grant's head.

Walter felt like he had turned to ice. Something was horribly wrong with Grant.

CHAPTER 15
Grant's Gift

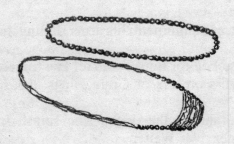

Walter couldn't move. He stared in horror at Grant. His fingers bit into the bark of the tree.

"Grant." He meant to call to his friend, but the name came out in almost a whisper.

His throat ached from fear. He swallowed painfully. "Grant!" This time it came out in a holler.

Grant kept floating.

Fear sent prickles down Walter's spine. He had to help Grant. Their fathers were too far away to hear him call.

He jumped down into the water, not noticing the cold or the water splashing into his face.

What if I can't help him? What if it's too late to help him?

Walter pushed away the awful thoughts. He'd do what he had to do. First, he had to get Grant's head out of the water.

The water wasn't very deep. It only came halfway up his drawer-covered thighs. He reached down and tugged at Grant's shoulders.

"Oof!" Walter stumbled back, losing his hold on Grant. Grant was a lot heavier than he'd expected!

He took a deep, heavy breath and tried again. This time he was prepared for Grant's weight. He tugged until Grant's shoulders were above water.

His chest grew tight with hopelessness when he saw that even though Grant's shoulders were above water, Grant's head was tilted back, letting water wash over his face.

Walter got down on his knees in the water, supporting Grant's head on his shoulder and pulling him slowly along toward shore. He tried to ignore the gash on the back of Grant's head that was bleeding on his own shoulder.

He dragged his friend onto the shore and dropped his shoulders. Grant's feet were still in the water. Walter lay in the sand and weeds for a minute, panting.

He's not breathing. The thought sent a terror like a flame of fire through him. *What do I do now? Show me what to do, God.*

A picture of Judith when she was two years old flashed into Walter's mind. She'd swallowed a button and was choking. His father had grabbed her, turned her upside down, and hit her on the back. The button popped out of her mouth, and she was fine.

Walter couldn't turn Grant upside down, but he rolled him onto his side and started pounding his back.

It seemed like forever to him, but it must have been only

a minute before Grant started coughing. He coughed water out of his mouth. Then he groaned and coughed some more.

Walter thought he'd never heard a sound as wonderful as that cough!

Grant groaned again and sat up slowly. Wincing, he put a hand to his head. He pulled it away, covered with blood. With a scratchy voice, he asked, "What happened?"

While Walter told him, he grabbed one of his socks from the pile of clothes. After dampening it in the lake, he washed the sand off Grant's wound. Then he rinsed the sock out, wrung it, and told Grant to hold it on his wound.

"I'll be back in a couple minutes. I'm going to get your father," Walter told him.

"I'm all right," Grant protested. "Let me put on my clothes and we can go back together."

He started to sit up. "Ooooh." He sat down again. "I'm dizzy."

"Stay here." Walter dashed back the way they'd come, not waiting to put anything on over his drawers. There was no one else but their fathers on that part of the shore anyway.

Later, sitting on a log, Walter glanced across the low burning fire at Grant. Mr. LaPierre had tied a piece of his own shirt around Grant's head, the white cloth looking bright against Grant's black hair.

Walter had thought their fathers would take them home right away after what happened, but they had said it would be wiser to wait. They wanted Grant to get dry and have something to eat before they headed back.

"How are you feeling?" Walter asked Grant.

"All right, except for a bad ache in my head."

Walter took the last bite of his helping of fried fish. "That walleye tasted great. Thanks, Mr. LaPierre."

Mr. LaPierre's grin shone out from his beard. "I'm glad you liked it, but I should be thanking you. You saved my son's life with your quick thinking."

Walter shifted on the log. The praise made him uncomfortable and proud at the same time. "Anybody would have done the same thing."

"You were the only one there, and you were the one who did the right thing. I am in your debt."

What a strange thought, that an adult thought he owed him anything! "Aw, I didn't want to lose my best friend, is all."

The next morning, Walter hurried through his chores so he could go over to Grant's house.

"How are you?" he asked when they were inside.

"My head still aches, but that's all."

"Good. I brought the newspaper."

They sat down at the wooden table in the kitchen. They never read everything in the newspaper. Instead, they read the headlines and the articles that sounded interesting.

That morning, they decided to read an article about an Indian tribe. A few minutes later, they almost wished they hadn't.

"The cavalry isn't satisfied with putting most of the Cheyenne, Sioux, and Winnebago Indians on reservations," Grant stormed. "Now they're going after the Nez Perce."

"I never heard of that Indian nation. Do they live in the Dakotas?"

"No. Their name is French for pierced nose," Grant explained. "They live in Oregon. Now the Indians are moving to a reservation in Idaho."

Walter frowned. "Are they being moved because they attacked white people?"

"The Nez Perce are proud that none of their people has ever killed a white man. Miners and settlers want the land the Nez Perce's reservation is on."

Walter read part of the article about the Nez Perce. "It says here that they killed eighteen white people this year."

"Yes. The Indian who led the raids was angry because a white man killed his father. Now Chief Joseph, the head of the Nez Perce, is trying to keep his people away from the cavalry. He knows the people will be punished for the killings."

Walter's heart felt sad for the Indian families and all they were facing.

When they finished reading the newspaper, Grant took a deep breath. "Father was right when he said you saved my life."

Walter fidgeted on his chair. "You would have done the same for me."

"You are a good and brave friend. I want to give you something, something you can look at every day and know I will never forget what you did for me."

Grant ignored his protests. "The gift is in the family living room."

Walter followed him. Their family living room wasn't as fancy and hadn't as many chairs as most Walter had seen. Walter guessed that was because only Grant and his father lived there, with no women to decorate the house.

Grant went to a small desk that stood by one of the windows. He opened a beautiful wooden box that sat on top of the desk, and removed something.

"My mother made this." With both hands, he held out a beautiful woven bead necklace.

Walter shook his head. "I couldn't take something your

mother made for you. She's dead, and you don't have many things she gave you."

"You saved my life. I want to give you the most precious thing I own. That is this necklace."

Walter hesitated. He ran the tip of a finger lightly over the beading. "It looks like it was made by Indians. Isn't your mother French?"

Grant didn't answer right away.

Walter looked up from the necklace, wondering why Grant didn't say anything.

Grant's gaze met his own evenly. "My mother was Dakota, a Sioux."

CHAPTER 16

The Secret

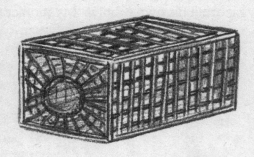

Walter couldn't believe his ears. "Your mother was a Sioux Indian?"

"Yes."

"That means you are—"

"A half-breed." Grant's voice was bitter. He stared at Walter, waiting for him to speak.

"I was going to say you are part Sioux, part Indian. Like I am part English and part Irish. I guess that makes me a half-breed, too."

"People don't hate whites for being two nationalities. It isn't the same."

Walter knew what he meant. There were those at school,

children like Robert, who would make Grant's life miserable if they knew he was part Indian.

Grant still held the necklace in his hands. Walter suddenly understood that trusting him with the secret that he was partly Indian was Grant's real gift to him. Walter could hurt him by telling the wrong people if he chose.

Walter reached for the necklace and slid it over his head. It felt heavy, but good, around his neck. "I'll keep it forever."

Grant smiled, and Walter felt like a weight had been lifted from his chest. He smiled back. "So your father had more than friends among the Indians, he had an Indian wife. No wonder you know so much about Indians. Did you ever live with them?"

"Yes, when I was very young."

Standing by the desk, Grant told the story of his life to Walter.

"For the first years after Mother and Father were married, they lived part of the year with her tribe, and part of the year they would spend alone with their own family while he trapped areas away from where her tribe was living."

"Their own family?"

Grant nodded. "I have a number of older brothers and sisters."

Walter was stunned. "I always thought you were an only child. Where do your brothers and sisters live?"

"After the Sioux Uprising, the Sioux were banned from Minnesota, remember? They were sent to a reservation outside the state."

"Yes, but—" Walter didn't know how to ask all the questions running through his mind.

"When they went to the reservation, our family went, too." Grant smiled. "Of course, I wasn't born yet." His smile died. "Father stayed with the family part of the year, and part of the year he came back to Minnesota to trap. There wasn't good trapping land where the tribe was sent."

Walter frowned. "I thought people who were only part Indian didn't have to stay on reservations. Why didn't your father keep your family in Minnesota."

"My mother wanted to live where her people lived: her own parents and brothers and sisters."

Walter could understand that. He'd heard Brita and Lars's mothers talking of the families they'd left behind in Sweden. And he missed Uncle Tim and his family from Cincinnati.

"When I was three, my mother died," Grant said. "That's when Father and I moved away from the reservation. My older brothers and sisters wanted to stay with the tribe and my grandparents."

"That sounds awful. My little sister, Judith, is a pest sometimes, but I think it would seem strange not to live with her."

"Father and I try to visit them at least once a year. This last year, we haven't been able to visit."

"Were–were people you know killed in the Indian wars?"

"Yes. Two of my older brothers fought in the battles."

The hair on the back of Walter's neck prickled. The thought of Grant having brothers who were caught in those awful battles made his stomach feel like he was going to throw up. "Were they. . .were they killed?"

"No, they weren't wounded or killed."

"It must have been hard for you," Walter said, "knowing about the battles and wondering whether they were still alive. And you couldn't even tell anyone you were worried about them."

"Father and I talked about them and prayed together for them."

"Where are they now?"

"Since they were only part Indian, they had to leave the reservation. They moved to the northern woods. They are trying to make a living trapping, like Father used to do."

"Doesn't anyone in Minneapolis know you are part Indian?"

Grant shook his head. "When we moved from the reservation, Father changed my name to Grant, after General Ulysses S. Grant, who became president. He told me not to tell anyone about our Indian family. He wouldn't let me speak Sioux, only English and French."

"How mean!"

"No. He did that because he loves me and knew how mean people could be to children who are part Indian."

Walter's stomach churned again. What would it be like to have to hide your mother's nationality? What if when people asked him about his own ancestors, he had to pretend some of them weren't real?

"Are you ashamed of being part Indian?" he asked. "I think you should be proud of it."

Grant's back stiffened. "I *am* proud! But I know one person can't fight all the boys at school who don't like Indians."

"Like Robert and his friends, who beat us up just for standing up for the Indians in class."

"Yes." Bitterness filled Grant's one word.

Walter fingered the necklace that hung around his neck. "What is your Indian name?"

"Little White Beaver."

"I like that. I'll keep your secret for as long as you want me to, Little White Beaver."

"Thank you."

"But I hope you don't have to keep it a secret forever."

Grant tried to smile, but didn't quite make it.

Walter and Grant continued to watch the paper for news of what was happening to the Indian nations. The Nez Perce's story made them sad.

Chief Joseph tried to take his people to Canada, where they wouldn't be forced to live on a reservation. His people traveled almost seventeen hundred miles. When the cavalry caught them, they were only forty miles from Canada.

Chief Joseph said, "It is cold, and we have no blankets. The little children are freezing to death. Hear me, my chiefs. I am tired. My heart is sick and sad. From where the sun stands, I will fight no more forever."

The leaders of the cavalry that captured Chief Joseph's people told him the Nez Perce would be sent to a reservation in Idaho, but they weren't. Instead they were sent to Indian Territory, a harsh land, where many died.

The day Walter heard what Chief Joseph had said, he looked at the sun and thought of the chief's words.

"If I were an Indian," Walter told Grant, "I'd rather fight until all my people were dead instead of surrendering to the cavalry and living on a reservation."

Grant shook his head. "I used to feel the same way. Now I believe it's wise for the chiefs to make sure their people stay alive, even if they must live on reservations where life is hard. Even if they must live in a way they don't like."

"Why?"

"When we studied the War Between the States in school, I asked my father why all the African people in America didn't fight against the slave owners before the war, even if it meant they would be killed. I thought it would be better to be dead than to be a slave."

"I thought the same thing when we learned about slavery," Walter admitted.

"Father said that if they had all let themselves be killed, their children and grandchildren and great-grandchildren would never have been born. If they had all died, there would have been none of their own people alive to remember they had existed. That would mean the slave owners had won the battle against the African people in America."

Walter thought for a couple minutes about Grant's words. "So staying alive and keeping their families alive was one way of winning the war."

"Yes."

"And it's that way with the Indians, too?"

"I think so," Grant said. "Indians may never again have the way of life they've always known, but maybe one day they will have the same freedoms as former slaves and white people. One day they may be able to choose where they will live and how they will support their families. They will remember the Indians who fought in the battles and tried to keep their ways alive."

How many years would that be? Walter wondered. It was hard to imagine a time when he and Grant would be old. Maybe it would take even longer, and their own children would be old.

Walter thought he understood what Grant meant. Still, he wished he could do something to help stop the hatred and fear between white people and Indian people. He wished there was something *he* could do to make a difference.

"If the Indian nations stay alive," Grant said quietly, "that is winning the war with the white people."

CHAPTER 17
Time for Change

Walter and Grant raced up the steps into the horse-drawn streetcar, paid their nickels for the fare, and dropped into a seat side-by-side. Their fathers followed more slowly. Behind them came Abe and his father.

Walter grinned at Grant, just from the sheer joy of knowing they were on their way to another ball match. This was the first one they'd gone to all year. It would be Abe's first one ever. The eight-year-old boy's eyes shone with excitement.

The streetcar bell clanged as the horses moved forward at the driver's command. The car jerked, then rolled along its rails.

"I almost forgot." Walter pulled a folded envelope from his trouser pocket. "A letter from Lars came today. It's addressed to both of us, so I thought we could read it together on our way to the ballpark."

Dear Walter and Grant,
 I hope everything is well with you and your families.
I miss Minneapolis and all the fun we had together.

Grant grinned. "His English was much better when he left Minneapolis last spring, but he still writes English better than he speaks it."

Walter grinned back. "I guess he doesn't have to worry whether *k*s are silent or *j*s are pronounced like a *j* or a *y* when he's writing."

They both laughed and turned back to the letter.

 Everything is going well on our homestead this summer. We've only seen a few grasshoppers this year. We think some of the eggs were frozen by the cold weather we had after the Day of Prayer. We've seen some strange little red bugs eating grasshopper eggs, too. Only a few grasshoppers are hatching.
 With the grasshoppers gone, settlers will want to live here again. The railroad company is planning to build a railroad to a town near our farm. I can hardly wait! Right now, the nearest railroad is over thirty miles away. All our supplies have to be carried by horse, wagon, or on foot over roads that are little more than ruts in the prairie. That is hard to get used to after living in Minneapolis! Father says we won't build a wooden house until the railroad is closer. It's

137

*too difficult to carry all the wood and other building
supplies over the prairie.*

Walter's father had told him the railroad was going to be
very busy building new roads. In addition to building supplies, he said railroads would carry new settlers to western
Minnesota and to Dakota Territory, where the Indians once
lived. The railroads would carry the settlers' grain and cat-
tle to market. It would be a good thing for both the railroads
and the settlers.

Walter didn't know how to feel about the railroads' new
business. It would be good for his father and the settlers, but
the railroads were not good for the Indians. He turned back
to the letter.

*Wish I could get to Minneapolis and go to a base-
ball match with you. The little towns near here have
baseball clubs, but none of the pitchers throws
curveballs!*

Your friend,
Lars

Walter wished Lars could be with them right then. Before
long, they reached the ballpark. Walter's heart started beating
faster right away. There was something exciting about just
being there, even before the match started. It was fun to listen to the men around them talk about the different players'
strengths and weaknesses and argue in a friendly fashion over
who would win or lose. There were so many voices that they
sounded like a loud humming.

Abe didn't want to sit down on the new bleachers. He
stood beside his father, his eyes wide, watching the kranks

and kranklets find seats and watching the players warm up for the match.

The Brown Stockings were playing the St. Paul Saints, from across the Mississippi River. The kranks always liked it when the team played the Saints. The newspapers kept up a friendly argument over which team was best, and so did the kranks in each city.

The game began with a roar as the first batsman, a Brown Stocking, hit a home run. The crowd filled the air with cheers and boos and hisses and hollers, depending on which team they were rooting for.

When Bohn, the Brown Stockings pitcher, got ready to throw his first pitch against the Saints, Walter leaned forward on the bench. It seemed to him everyone in the ballpark did the same, and like him, everyone seemed to be holding their breath. It was still like magic watching Bohn throw his curveball.

He didn't strike the batsman out this time. After three strikes and five balls, the batsman whacked the ball into left field. The Saints' kranks cheered as the batsman jogged to first base.

Walter and Grant laughed as Abe jumped up and down, yelling at the top of his voice. They weren't sure he even knew what he was yelling at, but he was having a good time.

Grant turned to Walter with a grin. "Remember the first time Bohn pitched here, against the Blue Stockings? Not one batsman hit the ball."

"I'll never forget it! But the Saints have played against him a few times now, so I guess they're getting used to his curveball a little."

When the teams changed places on the field, the kranks would stand up and stretch. Between the sixth and seventh innings, someone called, "Walter, Grant, hello!"

At first Walter didn't recognize the big man in the casual suit and bowler hat. Then Walter burst into a smile. "Captain Smith!"

The cheerful Blue Stockings pitcher stepped through a couple rows of chattering kranks and shook the boys' hands.

"I'm not a captain anymore," he reminded them. "The Blue Stockings have been replaced by the Brown Stockings, and I've been replaced by Bohn."

Suddenly uncomfortable, Walter shifted his feet. "I wish you were still playing," he said loyally. "You're a good pitcher."

"Yes," Grant agreed.

Smith crossed his arms over his big chest and nodded. "That I was, but not as good as Bohn."

"Don't you. . .don't you mind?" Walter asked.

Smith shrugged. "Life never stays the same for long. All things change. Bohn is better for the Minneapolis club than I would be as pitcher. The club will win more games with him, and the kranks will enjoy the games more." He grinned. "It's fun to watch him pitch, isn't it?"

Walter nodded. It *was* fun to watch him.

All things change, he remembered as Mr. Smith went back to his friends and the inning was about to start. Some changes were harder than others, though. Mr. Smith hadn't left the ball club because he wanted to.

Walter hadn't wanted to move to Minneapolis. Grant hadn't wanted to leave his family at the reservation. Children had to make lots of changes they didn't want to make. But he and Grant wouldn't be friends if they hadn't both moved to Minneapolis. Something good could come of changes, even if you didn't like the change. Even if you didn't have anything to say about it.

Walter had heard Brita and Lars's mothers talking about the changes they'd had to make when they left Sweden. There were many things and people they had to leave behind, but America offered other things that would be good for them and their children.

Grant leaped to his feet with a cheer as a player hit a ball. Walter peered between the kranks in front of him and watched the ball drop on the foul side of the baseline between home and first base. Grant sat back down, his gaze still on the field.

The changes the Indians were being forced to make seemed the worst, Walter thought. Those changes weren't happening because the Indians wanted them. They were big changes, and they would change Indians' lives forever.

Could anything good ever come out of those changes?

Grant turned to him when the clubs changed places again. "I almost forgot to tell you. Father heard that the cavalry officers who captured the Nez Perce Indians complained to the government about the way the Indians were treated."

"Because they were sent to Indian Territory instead of a reservation in the Northwest?"

Grant nodded. "They are going to be moved to a reservation in Washington Territory. It will be much better land."

Walter smiled, and Grant smiled back.

The crowd's yells started up again. The boys looked back at the field. Walter shaded his eyes against the sun so he could see better, and he remembered Chief Joseph's brave words: *The little children are freezing to death. . .From where the sun now stands, I will fight no more forever.*

Maybe now the children in Chief Joseph's tribe would have a chance to grow into men. Maybe none of the children on the Indian reservations would have to go hungry or be

141

cold. Maybe it would be good for them to have a chance to go to the schools the government promised to build for them. Maybe they would never again have to worry whether their fathers would be killed in battles.

Maybe someday, there would be peace and friendship between the Indians and the white people, like there was between him and Grant. Maybe Indians a long time from now would tell their children about the great Indian chiefs from the time of the Indian wars, like Chief Little Crow, and Chief Red Cloud, and Chief Rain in the Face, and Chief Joseph.

The sound of a bat against a ball brought Walter's attention back to the match.

It was a close match. The teams were tied for a long time. After the Brown Stockings had three outs in the tenth inning, Walter leaned forward with his elbows on his knees.

Beside him, his father whacked a fist into the palm of his other hand, over and over. "Come on," he muttered. "You can do it." Other kranks yelled.

The batsman already had eight balls and three strikes. One more ball, and he'd walk. One more strike, and the Brown Stockings would be out for this inning. And there were Brown Stockings players on all three bases, watching along with the crowd.

Walter held his breath as the batsman swung.

Crack!

The ball left the park like a cannon shot over the left-field fence.

The crowd rose to its feet with a roar. Walter climbed onto the bench he'd been seated on to see above the jumping kranks in front of them.

One! Two! Three! Four! The Brown Stockings players raced over home plate.

The crowd went giddy with excitement. They jumped up and down, yelled until the air seemed to vibrate from the voices. The bleachers shook from the stomping feet and jumping men.

Walter's father slapped him on the back, grinning the biggest grin Walter had ever seen. Then Walter slapped his father on the back. They laughed together and stomped their feet and clapped and yelled with Grant and Mr. LaPierre and Abe and Abe's father and all the other kranks.

The crowd didn't bother to sit down after that. The next batsman struck out, but it didn't matter. What mattered was whether the Saints would get four more runs against the Brown Stockings and tie the match up again.

The Saints didn't have a chance of doing that in one inning with Bohn pitching. One more hit was all they could muster.

The Browns' kranks were all smiles and good cheer as they left the ballpark. Following along with the crowd, Walter spotted Captain Smith grinning and shaking hands with Bohn.

Walter poked Grant in the side with his elbow. "Come on. I'll race you to the streetcar!"

Joy filled his chest as he ran. The sun was shining, his hometown team had won the match, and he was spending the day with his dad and best friend. It was pretty near a perfect day.

There's More!

The American Adventure continues with *The Great Mill Explosion*. Walter Fisk and Polly Stevenson are taking an evening walk with their friends Brita and Anton when an explosion rips through the air. Pieces of glass, wood, and concrete fall around them and black smoke rises above the mill where Brita's father works. Ten men are dead, and Brita's father is seriously hurt. Will Brita's father survive? And how can Walter and Polly help their friend if she has to leave school and give up her dream of becoming a teacher?